外語一點就會！

BIZ
E-mail+
電話英語

BUSINESS SKILLS:
E-MAIL AND
TELEPHONE ENGLISH

U0136635

發 行 人	鄭俊琪
出版統籌	李尚竹
責任編輯	盧亦珮
中文編輯	鄭瑜伽
特約作者	Timothy Daniel Ostrander、Ted Pigott
英文編輯	Helen Yeh、Mike Tennant
英文錄音	Mike Tennant、Laurel Bucholz、Helen Yeh、Doug Nienhuis、Meagunn Hart
美術編輯	黃郁臻、周秀圓
封面設計	鄭恩如
點讀製作	林育如
出版發行	希伯崙股份有限公司
	105 台北市松山區八德路 3 段 32 號 12 樓
電 話	（02）2578-7838
傳 真	（02）2578-5800
劃 撥	1939-5400
電子郵件	Service@LiveABC.com
法律顧問	朋博法律事務所
印 刷	禹利電子分色有限公司
出版日期	民國 105 年 5 月 再版一刷

外語一點就會！

BIZ
E-mail+
電話英語

BUSINESS SKILLS:
E-MAIL AND
TELEPHONE ENGLISH

LiveABC

英語數位學習第一品牌

目　錄

貿易活動篇

Communicating for Commerce

售後處理篇

Post-Sales Communication

用英語洽公沒在怕
E-mail & 電話溝通一本搞定

在全球化的經濟市場中，企業經常需要與世界各國的公司進行生意往來，企業員工自然也常會遇到接待外國客戶、海外出差，及處理國際貿易等事宜，因此英語成為許多上班族不能不會的能力之一。然而，忙碌的上班族並沒有太多自修時間，花錢上補習班充實英文實力往往又難以立刻見效。因此，本書針對所有上班族最需要的兩項英語溝通技能：E-mail 和電話來設計，將職場環境最常遇到的情境收錄其中，讓上班族能有效率提升英語溝通能力。

本書規畫 4 大主題，共 30 個情境單元，每個單元皆包括 E-mail 的往返和電話中的英語會話。其中，這四大主題是以實際上最常用到英語的情況，分成「人際關係篇」、「商務往來篇」、「貿易活動篇」以及「售後處理篇」，每個主題下再細分各種情境，讓讀者全盤掌握商務往來種種狀況會用到的英語溝通。

另外，在實際進入各情境單元學習之前，本書還規劃了「停看聽篇」，這裡告訴讀者應對往來的基本禮儀以及基本 E-mail 寫作重點與電話溝通基本技巧，你可以在這裡找到任何情況皆可能用到的實用句。在「英文 E-mail 不可不知的祕訣」中，我們依照「開場」、「正文」、「結尾」分類，你能迅速查到可參考的實用例句。而在「電話英語不可不知的祕訣」中，我們針對電話現場的接通到結束，整理出各種狀況皆可使用的應對句，讓你快速學會基本的電話應答。

接著，進入本書重點的情境單元後，你會先讀到每個情境一定要會的句型，接下來就是信件和電話英語範例，從閱讀的過程中立即學會這些商務常見的英語。

上班族平時工作已經相當辛苦，在努力工作力爭上游之餘，希望我們這本書可以讓你更輕鬆地加強英語溝通能力，提升職場競爭力。

本書共分 4 大主題、30 個情境單元，每單元都包含 E-mail 往返和電話中的英語會話，讓你在商務處理、各種業務作業以及辦公室人際往來各方面都能輕鬆順利用英語溝通。

一定要會的句型

單元一開始先列出此情境中會用到的重要句型，此句型在 E-mail 和電話溝通中都會用到。

E-mail 範例及回覆範例

每個單元情境下會提供一至三篇 E-mail 範例以及回覆範例。文章中會使用一開始教到的句型，讓讀者了解其實際應用的狀況。

UNIT 01 請假通知
Communicating a Leave of Absence

I. 請假一定要會的句型

✕ PLAY ALL ▌TRACK 010

句型1　告知請假時間

I will be out of the office for + 一段時間 + starting + 日期

= I will be out of the office for two weeks starting January 2.
從一月二日開始我將有兩個星期不在辦公室。

II. 用 e-mail 請假

✕ PLAY ALL ▌TRACK 011

To: Jane Anderson
Subject: Upcoming Leave of Absence

Dear Jane,

I am writing this quick e-mail to confirm with you that I will be out of the office for two weeks starting January 2. As I had mentioned to you earlier, I will be traveling to America for a family reunion[1] during this time. I will be back in the office on Monday, January 16.

I am currently working on a sales presentation for the Peterson Group, and Jason Su will be stepping in to handle my responsibilities. I am also involved in the preparations for the upcoming Design Expo in February, and Sue Peng will be responsible for these matters while I am away. In addition, I've talked to the other members of my team, and they are also ready to step up to the plate during my absence.[2]

While I am in America, you may contact me by cell phone at anytime. I will also be available

step up to the plate 承乏
「謀求棒又準」，如同棒球選手走上本壘板準備打擊。

via e-mail. My main contact in America will be my brother, Tim Lee, and his home phone number is (219) 462-6499.

Thank you once again for all of your assistance. I look forward to returning to the office on Monday, January 16.

Sincerely,

Mark Lee

中文翻譯

收件人：珍・安德森
主 旨：即將請假

親愛的珍：

我寫給寫下這封電子郵件是要跟妳確認，從一月二日開始我將有兩個星期不在辦公室。如同我先前跟妳提過的，這段時間因為要參加美國的家族聚會去美國。我會在一月十六日星期一回到辦公室。

我目前正在進行彼得森集團的業務簡報，蘇辭將接手我的職務並肩負我的工作。我也參與了即將於二月舉辦的設計展覽會的準備工作，我不在時彭蘇會負責這部分的事項。此外，我也和我組裡的其他人談過，他們也準備好在我請假時承乏工作。

我在美國期間，妳可以隨時打手機給我，也可以用電子郵件跟我聯絡。我在美國的主要聯絡人是我弟弟李提姆，他家的電話號碼是 (219) 462-6499。

再次感謝妳的協助。我將期待一月十六日星期一回到辦公室上班。

謹上

李馬克

1. reunion [ri`junjən] n. 團聚

2. absence [`æbsəns] n. 不在；缺席

補充資訊

文章或對話中有特殊的諺語或用法會特別用框框的方式加以解釋，幫讀者補充額外的英語及商業知識。

單字片語

文章中有重要的單字片語會特別列出來，標上音標中譯方便學習。

IV. 電話請假必備句

PLAY ALL | TRACK 013

告知請假時間

A: Will you be able to go over the new sales plan next Tuesday?

你下星期二可以看一下下週的銷售計畫嗎?

B: Sorry, but I will be out of the office for one week starting next Monday.

抱歉,從下星期一開始我會有一個星期不在辦公室。

A: I'm calling to remind you that I will be away on a business trip next week.

我打電話是要提醒你,下個星期我會去出差。

電話溝通必備句
此處列出每情境下,電話溝通的口語技巧,以兩兩對話的方式呈現,並標出重要句型。

電話溝通範例
讀者可從一來一往的長篇對話中,學到必備句的使用方式,並學到更即時的應對技巧。

中文翻譯
中文翻譯都直接跟在後方,方便讀者對照。

V. 用電話請假

PLAY ALL | TRACK 014

優先科技的業務代表吳珍伍打電話告知經理客戶,交代工作交接事宜。

Jane: Hello? Mr. Brown? This is Jane Wu from AdvanceTech.

你好?布朗先生嗎?我是優先科技的吳珍。

Mr. Brown: Hi, Jane. What can I do for you?

嗨,珍。有什麼為可以幫助你的嗎?

Jane: Well, I just wanted to let you know that I will be taking a leave of absence from the office for two weeks.

嗯,我只是要讓你知道我將會請假兩個星期。 **請假時間**

Mr. Brown: Thanks for informing me. When will you be gone?

謝謝你通知我。你什麼時候要離開?

Jane: I'll be leaving on January 30, and I will return to the office on February 13.

我會在一月三十日離開,然後在二月十三日回到辦公室。

Mr. Brown: All right. Who will be filling in for you while you're away?

好的。你不在的時候誰會代理你的職務?

Jane: My colleague, Fiona Wang, will be handling my duties for me while I am away.

我不在的時候,我同事王菲歐娜會替我處理。 **客戶端將代理人**

Mr. Brown: And in case of an emergency, how can we get in touch with you?

那萬一有緊急狀況的話,我們要怎麼跟妳聯絡?

Jane: You can always reach me on my cell phone or by e-mail. I've also e-mailed you an emergency contact number, along with the exact dates of my trip.

你隨時可以透過手機或是電子郵件找到我。我也已經將緊急聯絡電話,連同我旅行的詳細日期寄電子郵件給你了。 **緊急聯絡方式**

Mr. Brown: It sounds as if you've thought of everything then. Thanks again, Jane, for keeping me informed of your plans.

聽起來妳似乎已經把所有事情都設想好了,珍。再次感謝妳告知我妳的計畫。

48

49

為提供讀者們更多元的學習輔助，本書提供 mp3 音檔及點讀筆音檔（點讀筆須自備或另購）的線上下載。只要在 LiveABC 官網首頁 (www.liveabc.com)，依照以下步驟做音檔下載及安裝，即可開始使用 mp3 及點讀筆，方便讀者們邊聽邊學習。

MP3 音檔下載及安裝步驟

STEP 1
在 LiveABC 首頁上方的「叢書館」點擊進入。從左側分類中，點選「生活英語」的「英語隨身書系列」。找到您要下載的書籍後，點擊進入內容介紹網頁。

STEP 2
點選內容介紹裡的「下載 MP3 音檔」
> 下載MP3音檔 ，進行下載該書的 MP3 壓縮檔。
將下載好的壓縮檔解壓縮後，會得到一個資料夾，裡面即有本書的 MP3 音檔。

STEP 3
將下載好的 MP3 音檔存放於電腦或手機裡，即可直接播放本書內容，加強您的聽力學習。

點讀筆音檔下載及安裝步驟

STEP 1
在 LiveABC 首頁上方的「叢書館」點擊進入。從左側分類中，點選「生活英語」的「英語隨身書系列」。找到您要下載的書籍後，點擊進入內容介紹網頁。

STEP 2
點選內容介紹裡的「下載點讀筆音檔」
> 下載點讀筆音檔 ，找到您需要的點讀筆音檔後點一下，進行下載點讀筆壓縮檔。將下載好的壓縮檔解壓縮後，即能得到本書的點讀筆音檔。

STEP 3

用 USB 傳輸線連結電腦和點讀筆，會出現「LivePen 點讀筆」資料夾，點擊兩下進入「BOOK」資料夾。

STEP 4

將解壓縮後所得到的點讀筆音檔按右鍵複製，然後在上一步驟的「BOOK」資料夾裡按右鍵貼上，即可完成點讀筆音檔的安裝。

如何使用點讀筆啟動本書

STEP 1 將 LivePen 光學筆頭指向本書封面圖示，待聽到「Here We Go！」語音後即完成連結。

STEP 2 點 PLAY ALL 圖示，即播放整篇內容的發音，點任何句子，便可聽到單句朗讀。點 介紹公司 圖示，則可聽到重點句子的朗讀。

點讀筆功能介紹

- 內建高品質喇叭
- USB 2.0 傳輸埠 / 連接線
- 記憶卡插槽（隨機附贈 MicroSD 8G 記憶卡 1 張）
- 電池槽（2 顆 4 號電池）
- 3.5 mm 耳機孔
- 電源鍵
- 模式鍵　點讀　錄音　MP3
- 音量鍵
- 錄音孔
- 燈號指示　待機　點讀　錄音進行中
- 高感度光學筆頭

- 高科技光學點讀筆頭
- 支援USB檔案傳輸
- 內建高品質喇叭
- 點讀/錄音 MP3/字典 四機一體

尺寸	14.6 x 3.1 x 2.4 (CM)
重量	37.5g (不含電池)
記憶體	含 4GB micro SD 記憶卡
電源	4 號 (AAA) 電池 2 顆
配件	USB 傳輸線、使用說明書、錄音 / 音樂卡、字典功能版、micro SD 記憶卡 (已安裝)、產品保固書、保固回函卡

停看聽篇

在全球化市場環境下，e-mail 和電話是最常用的兩種溝通方式，也是許多人必須具備的職場技能。在我們學習如何面對各種不同情境的 e-mail 與電話溝通前，先來瞭解 e-mail 和電話英語的基本禮儀與必備用語，這些不但可應付各種情況，還可讓對方留下好印象。

I. 不可不知的寫作禮儀

✉❶ 主旨欄標示要清楚明確

主旨欄不可空白,並且要清楚標示來信目的,例如向對方詢問產品資訊,則最好要註明產品型號,可以採用首字大寫或標題的書寫方式,並且注意拼字是否有誤,若用全大寫或全小寫會容易讓人誤以為是垃圾信件。

 收件人有時會根據主旨來判斷其重要性或決定是否閱信,因此要簡潔具體。還有,使用 urgent 或 important 這類字眼要很小心,只有在非常緊急或傳送重要訊息時才使用。

Subject:

Subject: Product Information

Subject: Product Information Request:
　　　　Alpha Cement Mixer XC-191

Subject: Product information request:
　　　　Alpha Cement Mixer XC-191

❷ 簡潔扼要

商業電子郵件宜簡單扼要，只要將書寫的目的表達清楚即可，因此一些與公事無關的內容或寒暄皆可避免。不過，寄件者與收件人之間交情不錯的話則不在此限。

商業電子郵件中應避免寒暄用語或不相關的事情：

How are you?

How have you been? ❌

Hope you're having good weather. ❌

❸ 不要全部使用大寫字體

如果一封電子郵件全用大寫字體的話，感覺就像是 SHOUTING AT THE PERSON YOU ARE WRITING TO（對著收件人吼叫的感覺），會讓對方覺得突兀而對你的印象大打折扣，再者全大寫字體不易閱讀，會讓人無法將焦點放在信件內容上。

來比較下列這兩句話，就可以瞭解這個感覺：

I AM WRITING TO INQUIRE WHETHER YOU CAN PROVIDE YOUR LATEST CATALOG. ❌

I am writing to inquire whether you can provide your latest catalog. ✔

➍ 使用主動語態而非被動語態

可以的話，盡量使用主動語態。使用被動語態的句子看起來比較像是自動回信系統發出的訊息，而用主動語態的句子比較有人情味。

來比較下列兩個句子，主動語態是不是有較積極的感覺呢？

Your order will be processed today.

We will process your order today.

➎ 使用中性稱呼

在不確定對方性別的情況下，應避免使用單一性別來稱呼，也就是在表達時要留意語言的政治正確性。

不確定對方性別時可以用 they 或 he/she 來取代，或稍微調整句子，避免讓女性收件人有不舒服的感覺。

The client must sign in to his account to access his order summary. ✗

Clients must sign in to their account to access their order summary. ✓

The client must sign in to access the order summary. ✓

II. 不可不知的書寫架構

商業電子郵件不宜過於冗長，最好能在二、三個段落內將目的及需求表達清楚，以節省雙方的時間。

❶ 主旨

To:	Adam Horowitz
From:	MichaelDiamond@netmail.com
└ Subject:	Ordering Happy Pup Chew Toys

❷ 稱謂語 — Dear Mr. Horowitz,

❸ 主文

Following our phone conversation yesterday, I would like to place an order for your Happy Pup Chew Toys. I understand that the price for this product is $5.00 per unit. However, since I intend to start with an order of 1,000 units, would it be possible to lower the price? Please also let me know when would be the earliest I could expect to receive the products.

Thank you for attention.

❹ 結尾敬語 — Regards,

Michael Diamond

Ace Pet Care Supplies

✉️ ❶ 主旨（subject）

主旨欄不宜空白，需簡單說明此封信件的目的，例如：

▪ Holiday Notice	假期通知
▪ Inquiring about Tickets	詢問售票
▪ Prices that you requested	關於詢價
▪ Quote Update	最新報價
▪ Project Update	最新企畫

✉️ ❷ 稱謂語（salutation）

商務往來或正式的書信最好要寫出稱謂，如用「Mr./Ms. + 姓氏」來稱呼對方，若與對方熟識時，可直接稱呼對方的名字即可。若不確定收信者姓名時，可用 Dear Sir or Madam 來表示。

知道收信對象是誰時	不清楚收信對象是誰時
▪ Dear Joe,	▪ Dear Sir or Madam,
▪ Hi, Helen!	▪ To Whom It May Concern,
▪ Dear Mr. Brown,	

✉️ ❸ 主文（message body）

以簡潔為原則，通常包括開場（opening）、正文（body）、結尾（conclusion）三個部份。開場主要是表明來信目的、正文則清楚表明需求、結尾時再次表示感謝或表示願意提供協助等。

❹ 結尾敬語（complimentary closing）

基本上，收信人為首次往來的客戶或廠商時，應使用正式的結尾敬語。若是經常往來的夥伴則可使用非正式的結尾敬語。

正式的結尾敬語	非正式的結尾敬語
▪ Sincerely yours,	▪ Yours truly,
▪ Sincerely,	▪ Thanks,
▪ Best regards,	▪ See you soon,
▪ Regards,	▪ Cheers,
▪ Best wishes,	▪ Take care,

III. 不可不知的必備句型

❶ 開場

✘ PLAY ALL | TRACK 001

1-1 ▷ 點出來信目的

- I am writing to confirm the details of my flight.
  我寫信來是想確認航班的相關細節。

- I am writing about the meeting we had yesterday.
  我寫信來是想談談我們昨天的會議。

- I am writing to inquire about accommodation availability.
  我寫信來是想詢問關於住宿提供的問題。

- I'm interested in placing an order for your DVD series.
  我有興趣向你們訂購 DVD 系列。

- We'd like to invite you to our barbecue picnic.
  我們想邀請你參加我們的烤肉野餐。

- I am writing on behalf of my father, who is currently in the hospital.
  我寫這封信謹代表父親，他目前正在住院。

- I'm writing in response to your job advertisement.
  我寫這封信是回應你們的求職廣告。

1-2 > 訊息確認

- I am pleased to confirm that **your application has been approved.**
  我很高興向你確認你的申請通過了。

- I confirm that **I will be attending the ceremony.**
  我確認我會參加典禮。

- Just a quick note to confirm that **we have received your check in the mail.**
  只是簡單向你確認我們已經收到信裡的支票。

- This is to confirm that **we have shipped your order.**
  這封信是確認你的訂單我們已經出貨了。

- We wish to confirm that **your password has been changed.**
  我們要確認你的密碼已經更改了。

....

1-3 > 引用先前的訊息（信件或電話內容等）

- With reference to our telephone conversation today, I'm e-mailing you the contract to sign.
  關於今天在電話裡的談話，我會用電子郵件把合約寄給你簽訂。

- In my previous e-mail, I had mentioned the need to revise our plans.
  在前一封電子郵件，我提到計畫有修改的必要。

- As I mentioned earlier about next week's plans, we haven't yet decided what we'll do.
  就像我先前提到的，關於下星期的計畫，我們還沒決定要怎麼做。

- As indicated in my previous e-mail, I won't be in the office this Tuesday.
  如同我前一封電子郵件提到的，我這星期二會不在辦公室。

- As we discussed on the phone, I would like to close my account.
  如同我們在電話裡討論的，我想要結清帳戶。

- From our decision at the previous meeting, it appears that the company is making money.
  從我們上一次會議的決定來看，公司似乎有賺錢。

✉❷ 正文

✖ PLAY ALL | TRACK 002

2-1 提出要求

- We would be grateful if you could let us know if you're coming.
  如果你能讓我們知道是否會來的話，我們不勝感激。

- I'd appreciate it if you would respond before Wednesday.
  如果你能在星期三前回覆的話我會很感激的。

- I'd like to know if it would be possible to book tickets in advance.
  我想知道可不可能可以事先訂票。

2-2 要求確認

- Please confirm that you have received my e-mail.
  請確認你已經收到我的電子郵件。

- Could you please confirm that my order has been processed?
  可以請你幫我確認一下我的訂單是不是已經處理了？

❸ 結尾

✖ PLAY ALL | TRACK 003

3-1 若需其他協助

- For further details, please log on to our Web site.
  要知道詳細資訊的話上我們的網站。

- If you wish, we would be happy to send you our brochure.
  如果你想要的話，我們很高興將文宣小冊子寄給你。

- Please let me know if there is anything I can do to help.
  請讓我知道是否有任何我可以幫得上忙的地方。

- If you have any questions, please let me know.
  如果你有任何問題，請讓我知道。

- If you have any further questions about our graduate courses, please do not hesitate to contact me.
  如果你對研究所課程還有任何問題的話，請不要客氣儘快與我聯繫。

3-2 期待回覆

- I look forward to your reply.
  我期待您的回覆。

- I hope to hear from you soon.
  我希望不久就能得到你的消息。

- Please respond at your earliest convenience.
  請儘速回覆。

- Feel free to contact me by **phone or e-mail**.
  隨時透過電話或電子郵件的方式與我聯繫。

....

3-3 表達感謝

- Thank you for your help.
  感謝您的協助。

- Any comments will be much appreciated.
  任何意見都將非常感謝。

- Thank you again for **choosing our company**.
  再次感謝您選擇我們公司。

- Thank you for taking this into consideration.
  感謝您將此列入考慮。

- I appreciate any feedback you may have.
  您的任何意見回饋我都十分感謝。

- Your help with this would be much appreciated.
  您對此事的協助我們將萬分感謝。

- Your prompt attention to this matter will be appreciated.
  您對此事立即的處理我們將感激不盡。

❹ 回信者的開場

PLAY ALL | TRACK 004

4-1 表示感謝

- Thank you for purchasing our product.
  謝謝您購買我們的產品。

- Thank you for your inquery about our English summer camp program.
  謝謝您詢問我們英文夏令營的計畫。

- Thank you for your reply.
  感謝您的回覆。

- Thank you for your interest in our store.
  謝謝您對本店感興趣。

- Thanks for getting in touch with us.
  謝謝您與我們聯繫。

4-2 表示遺憾

- We regret to inform you that your loan application has been denied.
  我們很遺憾通知您的貸款申請被拒絕了。

- It is with great sadness that we share the news of our grandmother's death.
  知道奶奶過世的消息，我們都同感悲傷。

- After careful consideration, we have decided to sell our house.
  經過再三考慮後，我們決定賣掉我們的房子。

- I'm sorry to hear that you won't be coming this weekend.
  聽到你這週末無法前來，我很遺憾。

- I'm sorry to say that you did not win the prize.
  很遺憾要跟你說，你並未贏得獎項。

- Unfortunately, I don't have this information. I'll need to get back to you.
  很遺憾，我沒有這項資訊，我得之後再回覆你。

....

4-3 告知好消息

- It is my pleasure to tell you about our new products.
  能告訴你我們的最新產品是我的榮幸。

- We are delighted to let you know that your shipment will go out tomorrow.
  我們很高興告知你訂單明天就會出貨。

- We are excited to inform you of our latest offers.
  我們很興奮要通知你我們最新的出價。

....

4-4 抱歉未即時回信

- Sorry for the late reply.
  抱歉回信晚了。

- Sorry for the delay in responding to your inquiry.
  抱歉這麼晚回覆你的問題。

電話英語不可不知的祕訣

I. 電話英語必備句

☎❶接通電話

✖ PLAY ALL | TRACK 005

1-1 接通回應

非正式

- Hello?
  喂？

正式

- Doctor Lee's office.
  李醫師診所。

- Thank you for calling ABC Semiconductors. Selina speaking. How may I help you?
  感謝您致電 ABC 半導體公司。我是莎琳娜。有什麼需要效勞的嗎？

....

1-2 表明身份

非正式

- Hey Ellen. It's Mary calling.
  你好，艾倫。我是瑪莉。

正式

- Hello, this is Shelly Chen calling from Delta Designs.
  你好，我是三角設計公司的陳雪莉。

- Hello, this is Mary calling on behalf of Mr. Lin.
  哈囉，我是代表林先生打來的瑪莉。

- I'm calling from Taipei
  我是從台北打來的。

....

1-3 回撥

- Hello, Mr. Scott. I'm returning your call.
  您好，史考特先生。我是要回電給您。

- Ms. Smith, you tried to reach me earlier?
  史密斯小姐，妳之前要找我嗎？

- I'm sorry I missed your call this morning.
  抱歉，今天早上沒接到你的來電。

- I believe someone from this number called me.
  我想有人打這支電話找我。

....

1-4 找人

非正式

- Is Kate in?
  凱特在嗎？

- Is Billy there, please?
  請問比利在嗎？

- Can I talk to **your sister**?
  可以請姊姊來接電話嗎？

正式

- May I speak with **Mr. Oldman**, please?
  請問歐德曼先生方便接電話嗎？

- Would **the doctor** be in?
  請問醫生現在有空嗎？

- Could you please put me through to **Tom**?
  你可以幫我轉接給湯姆嗎？

- May I have extension **432**?
  可以幫我轉接分機四三二嗎？

❷通話中

✖ PLAY ALL | TRACK 006

2-1 本人接聽來電

- This is **she/he**.
  我就是。

- Speaking.
  我就是。

- This is **Mark** speaking.
  我就是馬克。

....

2-2 開場白

- Is this a convenient time to talk?
  現在方便說話嗎？

- Would you have a moment? I wanted to talk to you about **plans for this afternoon**.
  你現在有空嗎？我想要和你談談今天下午的計畫。

- I'm calling to **make a reservation**.
  我打電話來是要訂位。

- I'd like to talk to **Martha** about **the business trip next month**.
  我想要找瑪莎談下個月出差的事。

....

2-3 找的人不在時

- **Tim's** not in. Can you call back later?
  提姆不在。你可以晚一點再打來嗎？

- I'm afraid he's away from his desk.
  恐怕他不在位置上。

- **Jason** is not available at the moment. May I ask who's calling?
  傑森現在無法接聽電話。請問是哪裡找嗎？

....

2-4 忙線中

- **Tina** is on another call right now.
  蒂娜現在正在講電話。

- **Mr. Watson** is on another line at the moment. May I place you briefly on hold?
  華特森先生目前正在忙線中。可以請您稍待一下嗎？

2-5 轉接電話

非正式

- Hang on one second, please.
  請稍等一下。

- The line's free now. I'll put you through.
  電話目前沒佔線。我幫你轉過去。

- I'll connect you now.
  我將為你轉接。

- Just a sec. I'll get him.
  稍等一下。我轉給他。

「轉接」除了可以用 put sb through、connect sb 之外，也可以用 transfer、switch sb to 來表示。

正式

- Would you mind holding while I put you through?
  我替您把電話轉過去，請您稍等一下好嗎？

- One moment please.
  請稍等一下。

2-6 回電

請對方要找的人稍後回電

- Henry is on another line right now. May I ask him to call you back?
  亨利正在忙線中。要我請他回電給你嗎？

- May I ask Peter to return your call?
  要我請彼特回電給你嗎？

表示晚一點再回電

- No, that's fine. I'll call back.
  不用了，沒關係。我會再打來。

- When would be the best time to call again?
  什麼時候再打來最合適呢？

....

2-7 ▷ 留言

表示要幫忙留言

- Mr. Jackson is in a meeting at the moment. May I take a message?
  傑克森先生目前正在開會。要我留言嗎？

- I'm afraid he's stepped out. Would you like to leave a message?
  恐怕他出去了。您要留言嗎？

請留言給要找的人

- Yes, can you tell him his brother called, please.
  好的，請告訴他是他弟弟打來的。

- Thanks. Could you ask him to call Bob Morgan when he gets in?
  謝謝，他回來的時候可以請他打給鮑伯・摩根嗎？

- Do you have a pen handy? I don't think he has my number.
  你手邊有筆嗎？我想他應該沒有我的電話。

- Could you please have him call me back on my cell phone? The number is 0975-476-788.
  可以麻煩他回電打手機給我嗎？號碼是 0975-476-788。

2-8 確認訊息

- OK, I've got it all down.
  好的,我都記下來了。

- Let me repeat that just to make sure.
  讓我重複一遍再做確認。

- Did you say 353 Bade Rd.?
  你是說八德路三百五十三號嗎?

- I'll make sure he gets the message.
  我會確認他收到訊息。

2-9 打錯電話

- I'm afraid you have the wrong number.
  恐怕你打錯電話了。

- There's nobody here by that name.
  這裡沒有叫那個名字的人。

- There is no such person at this number.
  這支電話沒有這個人。

2-10 狀況 SOS

- Could you speak a little slower, please? My English isn't very strong.
  可以請你說慢一點嗎?我的英文不是很強。

- Could you please call me back? I think we have a bad connection.
  可以請你回撥給我嗎?通訊品質不太好。

> 聽不清楚的狀況包括:
> bad connection(收訊不良)、有 echo(回音)、interference(干擾)等情況。

- Could you please repeat that?
  可以請再重複一遍嗎？

- Would you mind spelling that for me?
  你介意幫我拼一下那個字嗎？

- Could you speak up a little, please?
  可以請你說大聲一點嗎？

❸ 結束通話

✂ PLAY ALL | TRACK 007

3-1 掛斷電話

- I have another call coming through. I better run.
  我有另一通電話進來。我得掛了。

- I have to let you go now.
  我得掛你電話了。

- I'll talk to you again soon. Bye.
  我們再聯絡。再見。

- May I call you back in ten minutes?
  我可以十分鐘後打給你嗎？

3-2 感謝來電

- Thank you for calling.
  感謝你的來電。

- Nice talking to you.
  很高興與你通話。

Ⅱ. 電話答錄機留言

❶ 電話答錄機

- Hello. You've reached 2957-3489. Please leave a detailed message after the beep. Thank you.

  您好,您撥的電話是 2957-3489。請在嗶一聲之後留下詳細的訊息。謝謝。

- Hi, this is Sandra. I'm sorry I'm not available to take your call at this time. Leave me a message and I'll get back to you as soon as I can.

  您好,我是珊卓拉。很抱歉現在無法接聽您的電話。請留言,我會儘快與您聯絡。

❷ 來電者留言

非正式

- Hey Richard. It's Jack. Call me!

  嗨理查。我是傑克,打電話給我!

正式

- Hello, this is Mike calling for Luke. Could you please return my call as soon as possible? My number is 2561-5689. Thank you.

  你好,我是麥克要找路克。你可以儘快回電給我嗎?我的電話是 2561-5689。謝謝。

電話英語不可不知的祕訣

停看聽篇

35

❸ 公司語言信箱

Thank you for calling Livetech. If you know the extension number of the person you wish to talk to, please enter the number now, followed by the pound key. Otherwise, please choose from the following menu: to speak to a sales representative, press 1; for technical assistance, press 2; for billing, press 3; for general inquiries, press 0. To listen again to the menu, press star.

謝謝您來電 Livetech 科技公司。如果您知道所找的人的分機號碼，請直撥分機號碼再撥井字鍵。否則請選擇下列的功能選單：業務代表請按一；技術協助請按二；繳費請按三；一般諮詢請按○；重聽選單請按星號。

Ⅲ. 電話號碼怎麼說？

✖ PLAY ALL ▮ TRACK 009

① 數字個別唸出

212-559-6970

♦ area code two one two, five five nine, six nine seven oh.

② 後四碼以「兩位數」為單位

516-848-7789

♦ five one six, eight four eight, seventy-seven, eighty-nine

♦ five one six, eight four eight, seven seven eight nine（較常見）

③ 美國免付費是 800 或 900

1-800-564-5544

♦ one eight hundred, five six four, five five four four.

在電視廣告或廣播中的電話號碼為連號時，通常不會個別唸出，不過一般人講電話號碼時，直覺上還是會一個一個唸。

416-888-1600

- four one six, triple eight, one six hundred（較常出現在商業廣告中）

- four one six, eight eight eight, one six oh oh（大多數人還是會這樣講）

人際關係篇

職場上除了一般業務往來之外，建立人際
友好關係也很重要，不僅可以拉近彼此之
間的距離，增加信任感，合作起來也會更
順暢愉快。好的人際關係首重真誠，無論
是祝賀、感謝、表達關心或弔唁，都要盡
快將你的心意傳達給對方，才能讓對方感
受到你的誠意。

請假通知
Communicating a Leave of Absence

I. 請假一定要會的句型

✕ PLAY ALL | TRACK 010

句型1 告知請假時間

I will be out of the office for + 一段時間 + starting + 日期

- I will be out of the office for two weeks starting January 2.

  從一月二日開始我將有兩個星期不在辦公室。

句型2 交代目前工作

I am currently working on sth.

- I am currently working on a sales presentation for the Peterson Group.

  我目前正在進行彼得森集團的業務簡報。

句型3 **告知職務代理人**

Sb. will be stepping in to handle my responsibilities.

- Jason Su will be stepping in to handle my responsibilities.
  蘇傑森將會介入處理我負責的工作。

句型4 **緊急聯絡方式**

You may contact me + 聯絡方式 + 時間

- You may contact me by cell phone at anytime.
  你可以隨時打手機與我聯絡。

II. 用 e-mail 請假

To: Jane Anderson

Subject: Upcoming Leave of Absence

Dear Jane,

請假時間 I am writing this quick e-mail to confirm with you that I will be out of the office for two weeks starting January 2. As I had mentioned to you earlier, I will be traveling to America for a family reunion[1] during this time. I will be back in the office on Monday, January 16.

交代目前工作 I am currently working on a sales presentation for the Peterson Group, and Jason Su will be stepping in to handle my responsibilities. I am also involved in the preparations for the upcoming Design Expo in February, and **告知職務代理人** Sue Peng will be responsible for these matters while I am away. In addition, I've talked to the other members of my team, and they are also ready to <u>step up to the plate</u> during my absence.[2]

緊急聯絡方式 While I am in America, you may contact me by cell phone at anytime. I will also be available

> step up to the plate 表示「著手做某事」，如同棒球選手踏上本壘板準備打擊。

via e-mail. My main contact in America will be my brother, Tim Lee, and his home phone number is (219) 462-6499.

Thank you once again for all of your assistance. I look forward to returning to the office on Monday, January 16.

Sincerely,

Mark Lee

--------- 中文翻譯 ---------

收件人：珍‧安德森

主　旨：即將請假

親愛的珍：

我匆匆寫下這封電子郵件是要跟妳確認，從一月二日開始我將有兩個星期不在辦公室。如同我先前跟妳提過的，這段時間因為家人團聚的關係我會去美國。我會在一月十六日星期一回到辦公室。

我目前正在進行彼得森集團的業務簡報，蘇傑森將會插手幫忙處理我負責的工作。我也參與了即將在二月舉辦的設計展覽會的準備工作，我不在時彭蘇會負責這些事情。除此之外，我也和其他組員談過，在我請假期間，他們也準備好會負責處理這些工作。

我在美國的時候，妳可以隨時打手機給我，也可以用電子郵件跟我聯絡。我在美國的主要聯絡人是我弟弟李提姆，他家的電話號碼是 (219) 462-6499。

再次感謝妳的協助。我很期待一月十六日星期一回到辦公室上班。

謹上

李馬克

1. reunion [rɪˋjunjən] *n.* 團聚

2. absence [ˋæbsəns] *n.* 不在；缺席

Ⅲ. 用 e-mail 回覆請假信

To: | Mark Lee

Subject: | Re: Upcoming Leave of Absence

Dear Mark,

Thank you for your e-mail regarding[1] your upcoming trip to America. I have noted the dates of your trip (January 2 to January 16). I have also noted that Jason Su and Sue Peng will be handling the lion's share of your responsibilities while you are away.

If any issues should arise,[2] I will be sure to contact you on your cell phone or via e-mail. I have also received your brother's emergency contact information in America.

> lion's share 這個片語是從寓言故事裡獅子分配到大部分的獵物引申而來，表示「大部分的、幾乎全部的」。

Once again, thank you for confirming the dates of your upcoming trip with me. Have a wonderful time in America.

Yours truly,

Jane Anderson

收件人：李馬克

主 旨：回覆：即將請假

親愛的馬克：

非常謝謝你來信提到美國行一事。我已經記下你的旅遊日期（一月二日至一月十六日）。我也記下蘇傑森和彭蘇在你不在期間，會幫忙處理你大部分的工作。

如果發生任何事情的話，我一定會打手機或是用電子郵件來跟你聯絡。我也有收到你弟弟在美國的緊急聯絡資訊。

再次感謝你和我確認即將去旅行的日期。祝你在美國玩得愉快。

謹上

珍‧安德森

1. regarding [rɪˋgɑrdɪŋ] *prep.* 關於

2. arise [əˋraɪz] *v.* 出現；發生

IV. 電話請假必備句

告知請假時間

A: **Will you be able to go over the new sales plan next Tuesday?**

你下星期二可以看一下新的銷售計畫嗎？

B: **Sorry, but I will be out of the office for one week starting next Monday.**

抱歉，從下星期一開始我會有一個星期不在辦公室。

A: **I'm calling to remind you that I will be away on a business trip next week.**

我打電話是要提醒你，下個星期我會去出差。

B: **Thank you for letting me know about this.**

謝謝你讓我知道這項訊息。

告知職務代理人

A: **Who will be handling the Thompson account while you are gone?**

你不在的時候湯普森客戶會由誰來處理呢？

B: **Ed Wu will be responsible for this account while I am out of the office.**

我不在的時候吳艾德會負責這位客戶。

A: **Cindy Ho** will be filling in for me **while I'm on vacation.**

我去度假的時候，何辛蒂會代理我的職務。

B: **Sounds good. Be sure to bring her up to speed on all your projects before you go.**

聽起來不錯。在你離開之前務必要讓她瞭解你所有案子最新的狀況。

. . . .

緊急聯絡方式

A: **In a worst-case scenario, how can we get in touch with you?**

在最糟的情況下，我們要怎麼與你聯繫？

B: You can always get in touch with me at **my parents' house. The number there is (444) 602-8904.**

你隨時可以在我父母家聯絡上我。那裡的電話是(444)602-8904。

A: In case of an emergency, please contact me at **the Bayside Hotel—(02) 344-7684.**

萬一有緊急狀況的話，請打到海灣飯店與我聯繫：(02) 344-7684。

B: **I'm sure everything will be fine, but it's nice to have this information, just in case.**

我相信一切都會沒問題，但有這個資訊不錯，只是以防萬一。

V. 用電話請假

Jane:	Hello? Mr. Brown? This is Jane Wu from AdvanceTech.
Mr. Brown:	Hi, Jane. What can I do for you?
Jane:	Well, I just wanted to let you know that I will be taking a leave of absence from the office for two weeks.
Mr. Brown:	Thanks for informing me. When will you be gone?
Jane:	I'll be leaving on January 30, and I will return to the office on February 13.
Mr. Brown:	All right. Who will be filling in for you while you're away?
Jane:	My colleague, Fiona Wang, will be handling my duties for me while I am away.
Mr. Brown:	And in case of an emergency, how can we get in touch with you?
Jane:	You can always reach me on my cell phone or by e-mail. I've also e-mailed you an emergency contact number, along with the exact dates of my trip.
Mr. Brown:	It sounds as if you've thought of everything then. Thanks again, Jane, for keeping me informed of your plans.

優先科技的業務代表吳珍在請假前打電話告知重要客戶，交代工作交接事宜。

你好？布朗先生嗎？我是優先科技的吳珍。

嗨，珍。有什麼我可以幫妳的嗎？

嗯，我只是要讓你知道我將會請假兩個星期。 請假時間

謝謝妳通知我。妳什麼時候要離開？

我會在一月三十日離開，然後在二月十三日回到辦公室。

好的。妳不在的時候誰會代理妳的職務？

我不在的時候，我同事王菲歐娜會替我處理。 告知職務代理人

那萬一有緊急狀況的話，我們要怎麼跟妳聯絡？

你隨時可以透過手機或是電子郵件找到我。我也已經將緊急聯絡電話，連同我旅行的詳細日期寄電子郵件給你了。 緊急聯絡方式

聽起來妳似乎已經把所有事情都設想好了。珍，再次感謝妳告知我妳的計畫。

I. 祝賀一定要會的句型

✖ PLAY ALL | TRACK 015

句型1 > **寫信恭喜**

I am writing to congratulate **sb.** on **sth.**

- I am writing to congratulate you on your recent wedding!

  我寫信是要恭喜你結婚了！

....

句型2 > **表達高興的心情**

I was pleased to + **V.**

- I was pleased to hear this great news from my colleague.

  我從同事那裡聽到這個好消息時感到很高興。

句型3 > **表達祝福**

I wish you ...

- I wish you both nothing but happiness in the years ahead.
  我希望你們兩個將來能過著幸福的日子。

II. 用 e-mail 祝賀新生兒誕生

To: Mary Oliver

Subject: Congratulations on Your New Baby!

Dear Mary,

I know that this must be a busy time for you. However, I wanted to write to congratulate you on the birth of your son this past weekend.

恭喜喜獲麟兒

I've been looking forward to hearing this good news for months. We've all been on pins and needles as the day grew closer. And now that your son is here, we are all so excited.

表達高興的心情

Motherhood is certainly very special, and I am certain that you will be a wonderful mother.

祝福新手媽媽

Once again, congratulations, and enjoy the new addition to your family!

Sincerely,

Cindy Huang

—————— 中文翻譯 ——————

收件人：瑪莉‧奧莉維

主　旨：恭喜喜獲麟兒！

親愛的瑪莉：

我知道這段時間妳一定很忙。然而，我還是要寫信祝賀妳上個週末喜獲麟兒。

好幾個月來我一直期待聽到這個好消息。日子一天天接近，我們也如坐針氈。現在妳兒子出生，我們全都感到無比興奮。

當了媽媽一定很不一樣，我很確定妳會是一個很棒的母親。

再次恭喜妳，並且好好享受家裡新成員帶來的樂趣！

謹上

黃辛蒂

Ⅲ. 用 e-mail 回覆祝賀

✖ PLAY ALL | TRACK 017

To: | Cindy Huang

Subject: | Re: Congratulations on Your New Baby!

Dear Cindy,

Thank you so much for your heartfelt e-mail. It was so nice to read your kind words.

Yes, it has been a busy time. But it has also been wonderful. Nothing is better than holding your own child in your arms as he sleeps.

Thank you again, Cindy, for your e-mail. I
can't wait for you to meet my son.

Sincerely,

Mary Oliver

─────────── 中文翻譯 ───────────

收件人：黃辛蒂

主　旨：回覆：恭喜獲麟兒！

親愛的辛蒂：

非常感謝妳令人窩心的來信。收到妳貼心的話語真的很高興。

是的，這段時間真的很忙，但是也很不可思議。沒有什麼比抱著
自己熟睡的孩子更棒的了。

辛蒂，再次感謝妳的來信。我等不及要讓妳見見我兒子了。

謹上

瑪莉‧奧莉維

IV. 用 e-mail 祝賀得獎

✖ PLAY ALL | TRACK 018

To: Tony Jenkins

Subject: Congratulations on Your Award!

Dear Tony,

恭喜得獎

I am writing this brief e-mail to offer my heartiest congratulations to you on the award that was given to you last weekend. It certainly is quite an honor to be named the Salesperson of the Year for your entire company!

表達高興
的心情

I was pleased to hear this great news from my colleague, Simon Zhang, who was at the awards banquet. I can't say that I was surprised to hear that you'd won, though, since you've always offered such great sales service.

祝福未來
成功

It's nice to know that I will be working with such a top salesperson, and I wish you many years of continued success in the future. Once again, congratulations, and enjoy your award!

Sincerely,

Harris Wu

收件人：東尼‧傑金斯

主 旨：恭喜你得獎！

親愛的東尼：

我寫這封短信是要為你上週末獲獎獻上我誠摯的祝賀。獲選為全公司年度最佳業務員無疑是一項榮耀！

我很高興從我同事張賽門那裡得知這個大消息，他當時就在頒獎宴上。不過，聽到你得獎我並不感到驚訝，因為你一直都提供非常棒的銷售服務。

知道我將會繼續和這麼頂尖的銷售員合作感到很高興，也祝福你未來能蒸蒸日上。再次恭喜你，並好好享受得獎的喜悅吧！

謹上

吳哈利斯

V. 用 e-mail 回覆祝賀

✖ PLAY ALL **|** TRACK 019

To:	Harris Wu
Subject:	Re: Congratulations on Your Award!

Dear Harris,

Thank you so much for your e-mail, and I'm sorry that I have not been able to get back to you sooner.

Actually, I was very surprised to win this award, since I work with such a great team of salespeople. It is quite an honor, though, and I am very grateful to have received this title.

Thank you once again, Harris, for taking the time to congratulate me on this award. I look forward to our continued cooperation in the future.

Sincerely,

Tony Jenkins

中文翻譯

收件人：吳哈利斯

主　旨：回覆：恭喜你得獎！

親愛的哈利斯：

非常感謝你的來信，很抱歉沒能早點回信給你。

事實上，得到這個獎我感到非常驚訝，因為和我共事的是一群優秀的業務團隊。然而，還是感到相當榮幸，我很感謝能獲得這項頭銜。

哈利斯，再次感謝你特地祝賀我獲獎。我也期待我們往後持續的合作。

謹上

東尼・傑金斯

VI. 用 e-mail 祝賀新婚

To: | Sally Strathers

Subject: | Congratulations on Your Recent Wedding!

Dear Sally,

新婚誌喜 I am writing to congratulate you on **your recent wedding!**

表達高興
的心情 I was so happy when I heard this good news.

新婚祝福 You and your husband are a perfect pair, and I wish you both nothing but happiness in the years ahead.

Once again, congratulations, and have a wonderful honeymoon!

Sincerely,

Melody Zhou

收件人：莎麗·史翠瑟思

主 旨：新婚賀喜！

親愛的莎麗：

我寫信是要為向妳新婚賀喜！

當我聽到這個好消息時真的很開心。

妳和妳先生是天造地設的一對，我希望你們將來能過著幸福美滿的日子。

再次恭喜妳，並祝你們蜜月愉快！

謹上

周美樂蒂

VII. 用 e-mail 回覆祝賀

✖ PLAY ALL | TRACK 021

To:	Melody Zhou
Subject:	Re: Congratulations on Your Recent Wedding!

Dear Melody,

Thank you so much for your kind e-mail. It was so thoughtful of you to write to me.

It was truly a special day, and it is one that my husband and I will remember for the rest of our lives.

Thank you again for your warm wedding
wishes.

Yours truly,

Sally Strathers

--------------------------- 中文翻譯 ---------------------------

收件人：周美樂蒂

主　旨：回覆：新婚賀喜！

親愛的美樂蒂：

非常感謝妳如此體貼的來信。妳真的很貼心還寫信給我。

**那真的是很特別的一天，也是我和我先生往後人生會永遠記得的
一天。**

再次感謝妳溫暖的婚禮祝福。

謹上

莎麗‧史翠瑟思

VIII. 電話祝賀必備句

✖ PLAY ALL | TRACK 022

祝賀晉升

A: I'm calling to congratulate you on **your promotion to vice-president.**

我打電話是要祝賀你升上副總經理。

B: **Thanks. I wasn't expecting to get it.**

謝謝。我沒有預期會獲得升遷。

祝賀交易達成

A: I heard through the <u>grapevine</u> that **you made a big sale this morning.**

我聽到謠傳你今天早上完成一筆大交易。

> 從 grapevine (葡萄藤) 聽來的，表示不是正式發布的消息，而是小道消息。

B: **Thanks, I did. It's nice that everything worked out.**

謝謝，沒錯，事事順利還真的不錯。

A: **Did you really <u>land</u> the DuoTech account today?**

你今天真的獲得二重科技這個客戶了嗎？

> 在口語用法中，得到工作機會可以用 land 這個動詞來表示，例如 land a job、land a role。

B: **I did. I've been working for months to get their business.**

是的。我一直努力了好幾個月才接到他們的生意。

....

祝賀新婚

A: **You and Sue make such a great couple. It was nice to hear that you finally tied the knot.**

你和蘇多麼的登對。聽到你們終於共結連理真是太好了。

B: **Thanks. We had a wonderful wedding.**

謝謝。我們有個很棒的婚禮。

A: **Hey, I've been looking for the chance to congratulate you on your wedding. Congratulations!**

嘿，我一直找機會要向妳新婚賀喜。恭喜！

B: **Thanks. It was the most magical day of my life.**

謝謝。那是我生命中最奇妙的一天。

祝賀新生兒誕生

A: **Congratulations on the birth of your daughter. How does it feel to be a father?**

恭喜你生了女兒。當爸爸的感覺如何？

B: **It feels great. It's amazing to look into my little girl's eyes.**

感覺很棒。看著小女兒眼睛感覺很奇妙。

A: **Nice to see you back at work. Congratulations on the birth of your boy.**

很高興看到你回來工作。恭喜你生了兒子。

B: **Thank you. He's such an incredible little guy.**

謝謝。他是個令人不可思議的小男孩。

IX. 用電話表達祝賀

Jenny:	Hi. This is Jenny Lai at Exeter Associates. Is Mark Lee in?
Mark:	Speaking. What's on your mind, Jenny?
Jenny:	I'm calling to congratulate you on the award you won last night.
Mark:	Wow. Word sure does travel fast.
Jenny:	Well, good news travels fast, Mark, and this is great news!
Mark:	To be completely honest, I never expected to be named manager of the year. I didn't even know I was in the running.
Jenny:	Come on, Mark. With the outstanding year your department's been having, this couldn't have come as a surprise.
Mark:	Well, it did. I'm just lucky to have such great team members working for me.
Jenny:	And we at Exeter are lucky to be working with an award-winning manager like you. Congratulations once again!
Mark:	Well, thank you once again, Jenny. I appreciate your taking the time to call and congratulate me.

艾賽特合夥人公司的賴珍妮打電話為他們事業夥伴獲獎獻上祝賀。

嗨。我是艾賽特合夥人公司的賴珍妮。李馬克在嗎？

我就是。珍妮，有什麼事嗎？

我是要打電話恭喜你昨天晚上獲獎的事。

恭喜得獎

哇，消息傳得真快。

嗯，馬克，好事傳千里，而且這是個大消息！

老實說，我從沒有料到會被選為年度經理。我甚至不曉得我在候選名單中。

拜託，馬克。你們部門這一年表現這麼傑出，這不是什麼太意外的事。

嗯，確實是。我只是很幸運有這麼棒的團隊跟我共事。

而我們艾賽特則是很幸運可以和你這位獲獎的經理一同合作。再次恭喜你！

表達高興
的心情

嗯，珍妮，再次謝謝妳。我很感謝妳特地打電話來為我祝賀。

表達感謝
Expressing Gratitude

I. 表達感謝一定要會的句型

✖ PLAY ALL ︱ TRACK 024

句型1 ▷ 表達謝意

I am writing to express my gratitude for sth. with sth.

- I am writing to express my gratitude for your help with our company's year-end report.

  我寫這封信是想對你在公司年終報告上所給予的協助表達感謝之意。

....

句型2 ▷ 給予回報

If you ever need my help, please + V.

- If you ever need my help in arranging these, please tell me.

  如果你需要我幫忙安排此事的話，請告訴我。

II. 用 e-mail 感謝業務協助

✘ PLAY ALL | TRACK 025

To: | Ken Lee

Subject: | Thank You for the Help

Dear Ken,

達謝意 I am writing to express my gratitude for your help with our company's year-end report. I really appreciate your assistance with this project. In fact, I don't think I would have been able to finish it by the deadline without your help.

予回報 If I can ever assist you in any way, please don't hesitate to let me know. I am always happy to help out.

Once again, thank you.

Sincerely,

Tom

收件人：李肯恩

主 旨：感謝協助

親愛的肯恩：

我寫這封信是想對你在公司年終報告上所給予的協助表達感謝之意。我真的很感謝你在這件案子上的幫忙。事實上，如果沒有你的幫忙，我想我是不可能在截止日期前完成的。

如果我可以在任何方面幫上忙的話，請不要客氣，儘管讓我知道。我隨時都很樂意幫忙。

再次感謝你。

謹上

湯姆

Ⅲ. 用 e-mail 回覆感謝

✕ PLAY ALL | TRACK 026

To:	Tom Yeh

Subject:	Re: Thank You for the Help

Dear Tom,

Thank you for the e-mail. Actually, it was my pleasure to work with you on the year-end report. I'm glad to know that my input was of assistance.

All right, Tom. Please let me know if I can ever be of help again.

Yours truly,

Ken Lee

中文翻譯

收件人：葉湯姆

主　旨：回覆：感謝協助

親愛的湯姆：

感謝你的來信。事實上，能和你在年終報告共同合作才是我的榮幸。我很高興我的投入有幫上忙。

好啦，湯姆。如果還有機會幫忙的話，務必要讓我知道。

謹上

李肯恩

IV. 用 e-mail 感謝演講安排

To: | Matt Smith

Subject: | Thank You for Arranging Yesterday's Guest Speaker

Dear Matt,

表達謝意 Thank you so much for **arranging** yesterday's guest speaker. I learned a lot from her presentation at the workshop. I hope to incorporate some of the speaker's tips here in the office.

The speakers and workshops that you organize are always very informative. 給予回報 If you ever need my help in **arranging these, please tell me.** I'd be happy to step up and help.

Thank you again for bringing in such a great guest speaker to our office.

Sincerely,

Katie Lin

—————— 中文翻譯 ——————

收件人：麥特·史密斯

主 旨：感謝安排昨天的演講嘉賓

親愛的麥特：

非常感謝你昨日所安排的演講嘉賓。我從她研討會上的演講獲益良多。我希望可以將她的建議應用在工作上。

你所規劃安排的演講嘉賓及研討會總是非常具有知識性。如果你需要我幫忙安排此事的話，請告訴我。我會很高興站出來幫忙的。

再次感謝你介紹公司這麼棒的演講嘉賓。

謹上

林凱蒂

V. 用 e-mail 回覆感謝

✕ PLAY ALL | TRACK 028

To:	Katie Lin
Subject:	Re: Thank You for Arranging Yesterday's Guest Speaker

Dear Katie,

Thank you for your kind e-mail. I was glad to hear that you enjoyed yesterday's guest speaker so much.

I enjoy organizing the speakers for our company's workshops, and it makes it all worthwhile to know that people in our company are benefiting from these events. If I ever need your help in the future with them, I will be sure to let you know.

Thank you again for the message, Katie. I look forward to seeing you at our next workshop.

Sincerely,

Matt Smith

中文翻譯

收件人：林凱蒂

主　旨：回覆：感謝安排昨天的演講嘉賓

親愛的凱蒂：

感謝妳友善的來信。我很高興聽到妳對於昨日的演講感到非常滿意。

我很樂意為公司的研討會安排演講嘉賓，知道公司同仁從這些活動中獲益就讓我覺得一切都是值得的。如果未來有需要妳幫忙的地方，我一定會讓妳知道的。

凱蒂，再次感謝妳的訊息。我期待在下次的研討會上見到妳。

謹上

麥特・史密斯

VI. 用 e-mail 感謝贈禮

✖ PLAY ALL | TRACK 029

To: Harriet Kresley

Subject: Thank You for the Gift

Dear Harriet,

表達謝意 I would like to thank you for **your thoughtful gift. I received it this morning at my office, and it really brightened up my day. In fact, I** have already received several compliments on your gift from my colleagues.

予以回報 I look forward to returning the favor in the future. **I can only hope that my gift will be as thoughtful and considerate as yours.**

Once again, thank you.

Sincerely,

Jeff Ma

收件人：哈利葉·克雷斯利

主 旨：感謝贈禮

親愛的哈利葉：

我是要寫信謝謝你貼心的禮物。我今天早上在辦公室收到了禮物，讓我整天心情都很好。事實上，我很多同事對你的這份禮物讚譽有加。

我期待將來能夠回報你。我只希望我的禮物可以像你送我的一樣體貼用心。

再次感謝你。

謹上

馬傑夫

VII. 用 e-mail 回覆感謝

✖ PLAY ALL | TRACK 030

To:	Jeff Ma
Subject:	Re: Thank You for the Gift

Dear Jeff,

Thank you for your e-mail. I'm glad to hear that you received my gift. I'm also glad to hear that you and your colleagues like it so much.

Actually, there is no need to reciprocate by buying a gift for me. I'm just happy to know that my gift was so well-received.

Sincerely,

Harriet Kresley

中文翻譯

收件人：馬傑夫

主　旨：回覆：感謝贈禮

親愛的傑夫：

謝謝你的來信。我很高興聽到你收到了我的禮物。我也很高興聽到你和你同事都很喜歡。

事實上，不需要買禮物來回贈給我。聽到我的禮物受到歡迎就讓我很開心了。

謹上

哈利葉‧克雷斯利

✕ PLAY ALL | TRACK 031

感謝業務協助

A: **I'm calling to say thanks for your help on the Patterson case.**

我打電話來是要謝謝你對派德森這件案子的協助。

B: **<u>Don't mention it.</u> I'm glad that everything went well.**

不用客氣。我很高興事情都進行得很順利。

> 表示不用客氣的説法還有：sure、sure thing、it's all right、it's nothing 等。

A: **Thanks a million for your assistance this morning.**

非常感謝你今天早上的協助。

B: **No problem. I'm always happy to step in and lend a hand.**

不用客氣。我隨時都願意參與幫忙。

感謝演講安排

A: **I just wanted to let you know how much I enjoyed the speech you gave yesterday.**

我只是想要讓你知道我有多喜歡你昨天的演講。

B: **Thanks. I hope that you picked up some information that will be of benefit to you.**

謝謝。我希望你能從中獲得一些有用的資訊。

A: **The guest speaker was very informative.** Thank you for **setting this up.**

這位演講人提供很多資訊。謝謝你的安排。

B: **My pleasure. I'm glad that you enjoyed the speech.**

這是我的榮幸。我很高興你喜歡這場演講。

....

感謝贈禮

A: I just called to say how much I appreciate **your gift.**

我只是要打電話跟你說我很感謝你的禮物。

B: **I'm glad you like it. I thought it would be perfect for you.**

很高興你喜歡。我就覺得它很適合你。

A: Thanks so much for **the thoughtful gift you sent to me this morning.**

非常謝謝你今天早上送我這樣窩心的禮物。

B: **I'm glad to hear that you got it and that you like it.**

我很高興聽到你收到禮物且很喜歡。

IX. 用電話表達感謝

Stan: Hi. This is Stan Hu at ComCorp. Is Sue Gordon there, please?

Sue: This is Sue. How are things, Stan?

Stan: Great, now that my project is finished. I want to thank you again for all of your assistance with this.

Sue: Oh, that's all right. I'm just glad that I could give you a hand.

Stan: You did more than that. <u>You saved the day.</u>

> save the day/situation 是指成功避免事情走向尷尬、不愉快、失敗的處境,表示「化險為夷;轉敗為勝」。

Sue: I wouldn't go that far, Stan.

Stan: No, it's true. I was really in a crunch, and I don't think that I would have been able to get that project in on time without your help.

Sue: You were on the right track. I just came in and helped speed things up a bit.

Stan: Well, I owe you one. So if you ever need any assistance with anything in the future, please don't hesitate to let me know.

Sue: Thanks. I'll be sure to let you know.

史坦打電話給蘇表示感謝，因為有她的幫忙才讓案子準時完成。

嗨。我是聯合企業的胡史坦。請問蘇·戈爾登在嗎？

我是蘇。史坦，最近怎麼樣？

很好，現在我的案子完成了。我要再次感謝妳在這件事上所提供的一切協助。　　　　表達謝意

喔，不用客氣。能幫上你的忙就讓我很高興了。

妳做的不只這些，妳讓我化險為夷。

史坦，我不覺得有到那個地步。

不，這都是事實。我那時真的是處境艱難，如果沒有妳的幫忙，我想我是沒有辦法準時完成這件案子的。

你的方向是正確的。我只是參與並協助讓事情進行得快一點而已。

嗯，我欠妳一個人情，所以如果妳日後有需要任何協助的話，不要遲疑，務必要讓我知道。　　給予回報

謝謝。我一定會讓你知道的。

表達慰問
Expressing Concern

I. 慰問一定要會的句型

✖ PLAY ALL | TRACK 033

句型1 得知壞消息

I am sorry to hear about sth.

- I am sorry to hear about this horrible disaster.
  我很遺憾聽到這麼可怕的災難。

句型2 表達同情

My deepest sympathies go out to sb.

- My deepest sympathies go out to you and the people of your country at this time.
  此時此刻，我對你以及你的國人同胞表達最深切的同情。

句型3 **提供協助**

If there's anything I can do for you . . .

- If there's anything I can do for you while you are recovering, please let me know.
  在你康復這段期間如果有什麼我可以做的，請讓我知道。

句型4 **給予祝福**

Our prayers are with **sb.**

- Our prayers are with you.
  我們會替你禱告。

II. 用 e-mail 表達對車禍的慰問

To: Molly Brown

Subject: Are you alright?

Dear Molly,

得知壞消息
I am writing this e-mail to make sure that you are all right after your recent car accident. I was shocked to learn this morning that you had been in a car crash a few days ago.

表達同情
My heart goes out to you. I know that the accident must have been a frightening experience.

提供協助
Please remember that I am always here for you. Should you need any support in any way, just let me know.

給予祝福
I look forward to getting an update from you soon. You are in my thoughts and prayers.

Sincerely,

Ken Lo

> you are in my thoughts 字面是表示「我會時常惦記著你」，常用於對方不如意時，希望藉此讓對方心裡感到慰藉。

中文翻譯

收件人：茉莉‧布朗

主　旨：妳還好嗎？

親愛的茉莉：

我寫這封信是要確認妳前陣子車禍後是否無恙。我今天早上聽到妳幾天前發生車禍感到非常震驚。

我對妳的遭遇感同身受。我知道車禍一定是非常可怕的經驗。

請記得我隨時都在這裡幫助你。如果有需要任何支援的地方，就讓我知道。

我希望能盡快得知妳的近況。我會掛念著妳並為妳禱告。

謹上

羅肯恩

III. 用 e-mail 回覆慰問

✖ PLAY ALL ┃ TRACK 035

To:	Ken Lo
Subject:	Re: Are You Alright?

Dear Ken,

Thank you for the e-mail this morning. Please don't worry—I am OK. I'm still a little shaken up[1] after the accident, but I was not injured. My car, however, was totaled.[2]

It's been a difficult time, and during times like these, it is nice to know that you can count on the support of your friends. Thanks again for writing me this morning.

Take care, and stay safe on the roads.

Best regards,

Molly

中文翻譯

收件人：羅肯恩

主　旨：回覆：妳還好嗎？

親愛的肯恩：

感謝你今天早上的來信。請不用擔心，我沒事。在意外過後我還是有點驚魂未定，不過我並沒有受傷。只是我的車子全毀了。

這段時間很難熬，在這樣的時刻，很高興知道有你這樣的朋友的支持可以依靠。再次謝謝你今天早上的來信。

保重，路上要小心。

謹上

茉莉

1. shake up [ʃek] [ʌp] *v.* 嚇到某人（常用被動語態來表示）

2. total [ˋtotl] *v.* 完全毀壞（口語用法）

IV. 用 e-mail 表達對手術的慰問

✖ PLAY ALL | TRACK 036

To:	Mavis Saples
Subject:	Get Well Soon

Dear Mavis,

I am writing to inquire about your health after your recent surgery. My colleague, Tony Nie, mentioned that you <u>went in to the hospital</u> yesterday for this surgery.

告知壞消息

I was sorry to hear about your recent health issue. I certainly hope that the operation was a success and that you are feeling better now.

> go to the hospital 表示「去醫院看病」、be in the hospital 表示「住院中」、be out of hospital 則表示「出院」。

提供協助

If there's anything I can do for you while you are recovering, please let me know. All

給予祝福

the best to you, and I wish you a speedy recovery. We will be thinking about you.

Warm regards,

Greg

收件人：瑪維絲·薩波絲

主　旨：早日康復

親愛的瑪維絲：

我寫信是要詢問妳最近手術後的健康狀況。我的同事聶東尼提到妳昨天住院動手術。

我很遺憾聽到妳最近的健康問題。我非常希望妳手術成功，並且漸有起色。

在妳康復這段期間如果有什麼我可以做的，請讓我知道。希望妳一切順利，早日康復。我們會一直掛念妳的。

請多保重

葛瑞格

V. 用 e-mail 回覆慰問

✖ PLAY ALL ┃ TRACK 037

To:	Greg Chu
Subject:	Re: Get Well Soon

Dear Greg,

Thank you for your considerate e-mail. I did indeed have surgery the other day, but I am feeling fine now. In fact, I'm feeling better every day.

It was nice to hear from you during my recovery. Your e-mail certainly put a smile on my face. Thanks.

Sincerely,

Mavis Saples

中 文 翻 譯

收件人：楚葛瑞格

主　旨：回覆：早日康復

親愛的葛瑞格：

感謝你體貼的來信。我幾天前的確動了手術，但是現在沒問題了。事實上，我覺得一天比一天還好。

在康復期間很高興聽到你的消息。你的來信的確讓我很開心。謝謝你。

謹上

瑪維絲‧薩波絲

VI. 電話慰問必備句

得知壞消息

A: **Did you hear about the terrible accident on the highway nearby?**

你有聽說附近高速公路上發生的嚴重車禍嗎？

B: **Yes, I just heard about it on the radio.**

有，我剛從廣播上聽到。

A: I just saw on Facebook that a hurricane hit Florida.

我剛從臉書上看到有颶風侵襲佛羅里達。

B: **Yes, you're right. Thankfully, we are all OK here.**

是啊，沒錯。謝天謝地，我們這裡一切都很平安。

....

表達同情

A: **Our boss just found out some bad news. He has cancer.**

我們老闆剛得知噩耗。他得了癌症。

B: My heart goes out to him and his family at this bad moment.

在這讓人難過的時候，我與他和他的家人感同身受。

提供協助

A: If I can do anything for you during your recovery, be sure to let me know.

在你復元期間如果有什麼我可以做的事，請一定要讓我知道。

B: Thanks. I'm sure I'll be up and on my feet again soon.

謝謝。我相信我很快就會再振作、重新站起來。

....

給予祝福

A: If it's any comfort, we are praying for you at work.

如果能給你安慰，我們會在工作時為你祈禱的。

B: Thanks. That means a lot to me.

謝謝。那對我來說意義重大。

A: I have a long and difficult road ahead of me.

我未來有條又長又艱困的路要走。

B: We'll be with you in spirit every step of the way.

未來每一步我們的精神都與你同在。

VII. 用電話表達慰問

George: Hi. I'm looking for Dottie Bender, please.

Dottie: Speaking. How can I help you?

George: This is George Karl at Excel Enterprises. Unfortunately, I have some bad news. Todd Pampalone was involved in a car accident this morning.

Dottie: Oh, my God! Is he all right?

George: Well, he's in the hospital right now. He'll probably be there for the next few days as well.

Dottie: I'm so sorry to hear this. I was just talking with him on the phone yesterday.

George: Yes, I know that he is your primary contact here at Excel. That's why I wanted to let you know about this right away.

Dottie: Thank you, George. I would have been wondering why Todd hadn't be in contact with me.

George: Well, if you require any assistance while Todd is recovering, please let me know. I'll be glad to fill in for Todd while he is in the hospital.

Dottie: Thank you. And please wish Todd a speedy recovery, if you see him.

喬治‧卡爾打電話給工作夥伴朵蒂‧班德告知同事出車禍的消息。

嗨，麻煩找朵蒂‧班德。

我就是。需要甚麼協助嗎？

我是伊克塞爾企業的喬治‧卡爾。不幸地，我有一些壞消息。陶德‧潘帕隆今早出了車禍。

喔，天啊！他還好嗎？

嗯，他現在在醫院裡。可能接下來幾天還會待在醫院。

我很遺憾聽到這件事。我昨天才和他通過電話的。　　　　　表達同情

是，我知道他是你們伊克塞爾的主要聯絡窗口。這也是為什麼我要立即通知你們。

謝謝你，喬治。我可能還納悶陶德為什麼一直沒和我聯絡呢。

那麼，陶德康復這段期間如果你們需要任何協助的話，請讓我知道。陶德住院時我很樂意暫代他的工作。

謝謝。如果你見到陶德的話，請祝他早日康復。　　　　　給予祝福

弔唁
Offering Condolences

I. 弔唁一定要會的句型

✖ PLAY ALL | TRACK 040

句型1 〉 **得知逝世消息**

It was with great sorrow that I learned...

- It was with great sorrow that I learned of the death of your husband.
  得知你丈夫過世的消息讓我感到相當哀傷。

句型2 〉 **表達哀悼**

Please allow me to express sth.

- Please allow me to express my deepest sympathy to you at this time.
  請容我在這個時刻向你表達最深切的同情。

句型3 > **緬懷逝者**

His passing will +V.

- His passing will leave a void in the hearts of those who knew him.

他的離去一定會讓認識他的人感到悵然。

....

句型4 > **表達慰問**

You are in my thoughts during + 時間

- You and your family are in my thoughts during this moment of grief.

在這段哀傷的日子我會惦念著你和你的家人。

II. 用 e-mail 弔唁

To: | Colleen McDurmott

Subject: | Condolences on Your Recent Loss

Dear Colleen,

得知消息　It was with great sorrow that I learned of the death of your husband. Please allow me to

表達哀悼　express my deepest sympathy to you at this time. I'm sure this must be a very difficult time for you.

Michael was a very kind and caring person.

緬懷逝者　His passing will leave a void[1] in the hearts of those who knew him.

表達慰問　You and your family are in my thoughts during this moment of grief. Please know that I am here for you if you need anything.

With deep sympathy,

Peter

收件人：珂琳・麥克德莫

主　旨：弔慰失去摯愛

親愛的珂琳：

得知妳丈夫過世的消息讓我感到十分哀傷。請容我在這個時刻向妳表達最深切的同情。我相信這段時間妳一定很不好受。

麥克是一個非常善良又關心別人的人。他的離去一定會讓認識他的人感到悵然。

在這段哀傷的日子我會惦念著妳和妳的家人。請記得如果有任何需要的話，我都會在妳身邊。

獻上深切同情

彼特

1. void [vɔɪd] *n.* 空虛；空虛感

Ⅲ. 用 e-mail 回覆弔唁信

To:	Peter Hu
Subject:	Re: Condolences on Your Recent Loss

Dear Peter,

Thank you for your e-mail. Your sympathy is appreciated.

Your words of support have been helpful in getting me through this difficult time.

Thank you again for your e-mail, Peter. It was good to hear from you.

Yours truly,

Colleen

中文翻譯

收件人：胡彼特

主　旨：回覆：弔慰失去摯愛

親愛的彼特：

感謝你的來信。我很感激你的慰問。

你支持的話語在我度過這個難關時幫了我很多忙。

彼特，再次感謝你的來信。很高興聽到你的消息。

謹上

珂琳

文化補給站

參加西方喪禮要不要包禮金？

在西方要不要參加喪禮是根據你與亡者（the deceased）與喪家（the bereaved）之間的親疏關係而定，並沒有一定的禮儀或法則。如果你覺得彼此的關係並不是那麼親近，則可以選擇寄送花籃、並附上親自書寫的弔唁信來表達慰問。

西方文化中並沒有白包的習俗，有時候喪家也會謝絕送花，而是請求送葬者（mourner）以亡者之名捐贈款項給慈善機構或公益組織。要留意的是，這種捐贈要在喪禮（funeral service）前七到十天之內完成，這樣喪家才能將捐贈名冊公布於喪禮上。而進行捐贈時，捐贈人要確認受贈機構知道喪家名諱及住址，這樣才能告知喪家有這筆捐贈，而捐贈者可以在弔唁信上表明有此捐贈，但無須提到捐贈金額。

弔唁相關的補充單字

弔唁：express/offer/send condolences

哀慟：mourn、grieve

祈禱：pray

去世：die

過世：pass away（較委婉的說法）

恢復：get over、recover from

一直惦念著某人：be thinking of sb.

一切安好：wish sb. peace

悲傷：sorrow、grief

令人尊敬的：respected

善良的：kind

慷慨的：generous

Ⅳ. 電話弔唁必備句

✖ PLAY ALL | TRACK 043

得知逝世消息

A: I was sorry to hear about the recent death in your family.

我很遺憾聽到最近你家人過世的消息。

B: Thank you. It has been a difficult time for all of us.

謝謝。對我們家人而言這段日子很不好受。

A: I am grief-stricken over the death of your husband.

對於妳丈夫的逝世我感到極為悲痛。

B: Yes, it was totally unexpected.

是啊，這完全出乎意料之外。

表達哀悼

A: Please accept our condolences on this sad event.

請接受我們對此悲傷事件的哀悼之意。

B: We certainly appreciate it.

我們相當感激。

A: You have our sincere condolences.

我們向你表達誠摯的慰問之意。

B: Thank you very much.

非常感謝你們。

緬懷逝者

A: **Candice** will be sadly missed by all. **Her presence brought a smile to the face of everyone who knew her.**

坎蒂絲將讓我們所有人難過地想念她。她在的時候為每一位認識她的人帶來歡樂。

B: Thank you. I appreciate your kind words.

謝謝你。我很感激你善意的話語。

給予協助

A: If there's any way I can help you through this difficult moment, just tell me.

如果有可能幫上忙讓你熬過這段日子的地方，儘管告訴我。

B: **Your thoughts mean a lot to me.**

你的關懷對我來説很重要。

表達慰問

A: I wish you peace as you grieve the loss of your loved one.

我希望你在為失去所愛而感到哀傷時一切都安好。

B: Thank you.

謝謝你。

V. 用電話弔唁

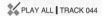

PLAY ALL | TRACK 044

Fred: Hello. Is Helen there, please?

Helen: Yes, this is Helen.

Fred: Helen, this is Fred over at Amcro. I'm calling because I just learned of the recent loss in your family.

Helen: Oh, yes. It was very unexpected.

Fred: Well, I was sad to hear this news. You have my complete sympathy.

Helen: It has been a difficult time for us.

Fred: If there is anything I can do for you at this time, please don't hesitate to let me know.

Helen: Thank you. I think I'll be able to manage.

Fred: Well, I wish you peace as you grieve over your loss.

Helen: Thank you, Fred. That means a lot.

弗萊德得知工作夥伴海倫失去至親的消息，打電話向她表達慰問之意。

你好。請問海倫在嗎？

是，我就是海倫。

海倫，我是艾莫科的弗萊德。我打來是因為聽到最近妳家人過世的消息。　　　　　　得知消息

喔，是啊。這件事出乎意料之外。

嗯，我很難過聽到這個消息，對此我深表同情。　　　　表達哀悼

發生這個事情以來，我們都很難過。

這段時間如果有什麼我可以幫得上忙的地方，請讓我知道。

謝謝。我想我可以應付得來。

那麼，我希望妳在哀悼失去所愛時一切安好。　　　表達慰問

謝謝你，弗萊德。那對我來說很重要。

I. 邀請一定要會的句型

✖ PLAY ALL | TRACK 045

句型1 **活動時間地點**

You are cordially invited to + 活動 + on 日期 + at 時間 + at 地點

- You are cordially invited to my son's upcoming wedding on February 6, 2016, at 2 p.m. at the Northside Methodist Church.

  誠摯地邀請你參加小犬的婚禮，時間、地點謹訂於二〇一六年二月六日下午兩點於北方衛理教堂舉行。

....

句型2 **注意事項**

Please note that S. + V.

- Please note that the dress code is semiformal.

  請留意需穿著半正式的服裝。

句型3 〉 **交通位置**

Sth. is located at/in + 地方

- Northside Methodist Church is located at the corner of State Street and Fallstaff Drive.
  北方衛理教堂位於史塔特街與弗斯塔夫大道轉角處。

....

句型4 〉 **歡迎蒞臨**

We look forward to + V-ing.

- We look forward to seeing you on this special day.
  我們期盼在這個特別的日子能見到你。

II. 用 e-mail 邀請參加婚禮

To:	Tom Peterson
Subject:	Wedding Invitation

Dear Tom,

活動時間
地點

You are cordially invited to my son's upcoming wedding on February 6, 2016, at 2 p.m. at the Northside Methodist Church.

We would be very happy if you could take part in this joyous event, and we extend this invitation also to your family.

注意事項

Please note that the dress code is semiformal.

交通位置

Northside Methodist Church is located at the corner of State Street and Fallstaff Drive. Parking is available nearby. A map and detailed directions can be found at this link: Northside Methodist Church.

歡迎蒞臨

You can contact me by phone or e-mail to confirm your attendance. We look forward to seeing you on this special day.

Sincerely,

Helen

收件人：湯姆‧彼特森

主　旨：婚禮邀請

親愛的湯姆：

誠摯地邀請你參加小犬的婚禮，時間、地點謹訂於二〇一六年二月六日下午兩點於北方衛理教堂舉行。

若你能來參加這個喜事我們會感到非常高興，我們也同樣邀請你的家人參加。

請留意需穿著半正式的服裝。

北方衛理教堂位於史塔特街與弗斯塔夫大道轉角處。附近有停車位。地圖和詳細的方位請見此連結：Northside Methodist Church。

你可以用電話或電子郵件跟我聯絡確認是否出席。我們期盼在這個特別的日子能見到你。

謹上

海倫

Ⅲ. 用 e-mail 回覆邀請

✖ PLAY ALL | TRACK 047

To:	Helen Lu
Subject:	Re: Wedding Invitation

Dear Helen,

Thank you for your e-mail. Congratulations on your son's upcoming wedding!

My wife and I would be delighted to attend.

Thank you once again.

Yours truly,

Tom

中文翻譯

收件人：盧海倫

主　旨：回覆：婚禮邀請

親愛的海倫：

感謝妳的來信。恭喜妳兒子即將舉行婚禮！

我太太和我很樂意參加。

再次感謝妳。

謹上

湯姆

IV. 用 e-mail 邀請參加聖誕派對

✖ PLAY ALL | TRACK 048

To:	Ken Kersey
Subject:	Christmas Party Invitation

Dear Ken,

活動時間
地點

Amtex will be hosting a Christmas party on December 23 at Tower Hotel, and we would be honored if you could come and join us. Company staff, along with many of our valued customers and suppliers, will be attending.

Drinks and appetizers will be served at 6 p.m., and a sit-down dinner will begin at 7 p.m.

交通位置

The Tower Hotel is located at **246 Seaside Avenue.** For your convenience, here is a link to a map with the exact address along with detailed directions: <u>Tower Hotel</u>.

歡迎蒞臨

We certainly hope you can make it. **Please RSVP** when you get a chance.

> RSVP 為法語 repondez s'il vous plait 的縮寫，常用在邀請函中，表示希望能得到回覆的意思。

Sincerely,

Paul

收件人：肯恩 · 柯爾西

主　旨：聖誕派對邀請

親愛的肯恩：

艾姆泰克斯將於十二月二十三日在淘兒飯店舉辦聖誕派對，如果你能來共襄盛舉將是我們的榮幸。公司員工以及我們許多重要客戶和供應商都將會參加。

飲料及開胃點心會在晚上六點供應，正式晚宴將於七點開始。

淘兒飯店位於海濱路二四六號。為了你的方便，這裡附上地圖連結 Tower Hotel，上面有確切的地址以及詳細方位。

我們非常希望你能赴宴。有空請回覆是否參加。

謹上

保羅

V. 用 e-mail 回覆邀請

✖ PLAY ALL ▍TRACK 049

To:	Paul Zhang
Subject:	Re: Christmas Party Invitation

Dear Paul,

Thank you for you the e-mail. Thank you, too, for the invitation to your company's Christmas party on December 23.

My wife and I are planning to attend. Please put us down for two people.

Thank you once again. Happy holidays!

Yours truly,

Ken

──────── 中文翻譯 ────────

收件人：張保羅

主　旨：回覆：聖誕派對邀請

親愛的保羅：

感謝你的來信。也感謝你邀請我參加你們公司十二月二十三日的聖誕派對。

我太太和我都打算參加。請幫我們登記兩位。

再次感謝你。佳節愉快！

謹上

肯恩

VI. 用 e-mail 邀請參加生日派對

| To: | Sarah Owens |
| Subject: | Birthday Party Invitation |

Dear Sarah,

活動時間地點

I would like to invite you to my birthday party, which will be held on Friday, December 10, at 7 p.m. at my apartment. Many of my coworkers and friends will be attending.

注意事項

It's not necessary to bring a gift, but if you'd like to bring something to eat or drink, please do.

交通位置

My apartment is located in the Chapel Manor neighborhood. Please find attached a map with my exact address along with detailed directions: Gail's Apartment.

歡迎蒞臨

I hope to see you at the party.

Sincerely,

Gail

收件人：莎拉‧歐文斯

主　旨：生日派對邀請

親愛的莎拉：

我想要邀請妳來參加我的生日派對，訂於十二月十日星期五晚上七點在我的公寓舉行。我的許多同事和朋友都會參加。

不需要帶禮物，但是如果妳想帶一些東西來吃喝的話，請便。

我的公寓在教堂莊園社區裡。請見附件 Gail's Apartment 裡的地圖，裡頭有我確切的地址以及詳細的方位。

我希望能在派對上見到妳。

謹上

蓋兒

VII. 電話邀請必備句

活動時間地點

A: **The party will be held on Friday night at 7 p.m.**

派對會在星期五晚上七點舉行。

B: **I look forward to being there.**

我很期待出席。

A: **The wedding will take place next month at the Catholic Church.**

婚禮將在下個月於天主教堂舉行。

B: **Great. Do you know the time and the date of the wedding?**

太棒了。你知道婚禮的時間跟日期嗎？

....

注意事項

A: **The dress code for the party will be formal.**

須穿著正式服裝出席派對。

B: **Thank you. That's good to know.**

謝謝。很高興知道這件事。

A: **Please feel free to bring some food or drinks to the party.**

想帶一些食物和飲料來參加派對的話請自便。

B: **That's a great idea. I'll bring my famous curry.**

那是個好主意。我會帶我最有名的咖哩。

交通位置

A: **Here is a map with detailed directions to the event.**

這裡是一份活動會場詳細方位的地圖。

B: **Thanks. This is very useful.**

謝謝。這非常有用。

歡迎菈臨

A: **Thanks for inviting me to your party.**

謝謝你邀請我參加派對。

B: **Well, I certainly hope to see you there.**

嗯,我非常希望能在那裡看到你。

VIII. 用電話邀請

Denise: Hi, I'd like to speak to Hal Parsons, please.

Hal: This is Hal. Is this Denise Waitley?

Denise: It sure is. I'm calling to invite you to my birthday party.

Hal: Thanks, Denise. Where and when will it be?

Denise: The party will be at my house, this coming Friday, at 7:00 p.m.

Hal: Sounds good. I'm sure I can make it. Is there something in particular you'd like me to bring?

Denise: If you'd like, you could bring a bottle of wine, but it's really not necessary to bring a gift.

Hal: Could you remind me where you live?

Denise: I'll send you an e-mail this evening with my address and driving directions.

Hal: Great. Thanks again, Denise. I'll see you at the party.

丹妮絲打電話給豪爾，邀請他來參加她的生日派對。

嗨，麻煩一下我要找豪爾‧帕森斯。

我是豪爾。妳是丹妮絲‧維特利嗎？

是的。我打電話是要邀請你來參加我的生日派對。

謝謝妳，丹妮絲。是在什麼地方跟什麼時候呢？

派對在我家舉行，在這個星期五晚上七點。

活動時間
地點

聽起來不錯。我確定能參加。妳要我帶什麼特別的東西嗎？

如果你要的話，可以帶一瓶紅酒，不過真的不需要帶禮物。

注意事項

妳可以提醒我妳家在哪裡嗎？

今晚我會寄電子郵件給你，上面會有我的地址跟行車路線。

交通位置

太好了。再次感謝妳，丹妮絲。派對上見。

商務往來篇

在第七至第十二單元中我們將介紹一般商務往來會遇到的狀況，這類的信件或電話用語目的是要與對方確認即將進行的拜訪、參展等活動，溝通時以簡單扼要為主。而第十三至第十五單元則為要求代理權、著作權許可、告知新的業務關係等情況，需多留意專有名詞以及合約細節的說法。

展開業務關係
Starting a Business Relationship

I. 展開業務關係一定要會的句型

✖ PLAY ALL | TRACK 053

句型1 **介紹公司**

We produce sth.（產品）with sth.（技術）

- We produce custom-built LCD screens with our state-of-the-art manufacturing facilities here in Taiwan.

  我們用台灣這裡最先進的生產設備製造客製化液晶螢幕。

句型2 **銷售量**

Our sales volume surpassed/ exceeded + 數量 + 時間

- Our sales volume surpassed one million units last year, making us the largest supplier of LCD screens in the region.

  我們去年銷售量遠超過一百萬台,使我們成為本地液晶螢幕最大的供應商。

句型3 > **公司優勢**

You should know that S. + V.

- You should know that we have a reputation for service and reliability.
  您應該要知道的是我們在服務以及信賴度方面享有盛名。

....

句型4 > **期盼合作**

. . . we invite you to be part of our success.

- Our business is growing fast and we invite you to be part of our success.
  我們的事業突飛猛進，歡迎您和我們一起共創成功的未來。

II. 用 e-mail 展開業務關係

To: | Greg Reynolds

Subject: | Hello from Royal LCD

Dear Mr. Reynolds,

Brad Cooper, our mutual business associate over at Upim Technologies, suggested that I contact you to let you know about my company, Royal LCD. We 介紹公司 produce custom-built LCD screens with our state-of-the-art manufacturing facilities here in Taiwan.

> state-of-the-art 用來形容當下最先進技術的設備或科技。

Royal LCD is a leader in the touch screen market. We have earned the respect of local and international companies by our attention to detail and high standards. We believe our finished product should be exactly what our clients order and free of 銷售量 defects. Our sales volume surpassed one million units last year, making us the largest supplier of LCD screens in the region.

公司優勢 You should know that we have a reputation for service and reliability. When working with Royal LCD you can expect to receive "The Royal Treatment." All our clients benefit from the attention to detail their order deserves. Please feel free to browse

through our Web site at www.royal-lcd.com.
tw for more information.

殷盼合作

Our business is growing fast and we invite
you to be a part of our success. Limitless
Technologies can enjoy the advantages
of high-quality LCD screens produced the
Royal way. Our testing facilities ensure the
finished product will perform as expected.

Thank you for taking the time to consider
Royal LCD. Should you have any questions
or would like a product demonstration,
please do not hesitate to contact me.

Sincerely,

Paul Wang
Royal LCD

中文翻譯

收件人：葛瑞格‧雷諾茲

主　旨：皇家液晶顯示器向您問候

雷諾茲先生您好：

我們在優平科技共同的商業夥伴布萊德‧庫柏，建議我和您聯繫，讓您瞭解敝公司皇家液晶顯示器。我們用台灣這裡最先進的生產設備製造客製化的液晶螢幕。

皇家液晶顯示器是觸控式螢幕市場的龍頭。我們以注重細節及對高標準的要求而獲得國內外公司的推崇。我們相信我們的成品絕對符合客戶需求並且品質無虞。我們去年銷售量遠超過一百萬台，使我們成為本地液晶螢幕最大的供應商。

您應該要知道的是我們在服務及信賴度方面享有盛名。與皇家

液晶螢幕顯示器合作,您可以預期能得到「皇家般的禮遇」。我們所有客戶皆因我們對商品細節用心而受益。想瞭解更多的訊息,歡迎隨時至我們網站(www.royal-lcd.com.tw)瀏覽。

我們的事業突飛猛進,歡迎您和我們一起共創成功的未來。無限科技可以享受到皇家生產製造的高品質液晶顯示器帶來的好處。我們的測試設備確保成品表現會與預期相同。

感謝您撥冗考慮皇家液晶顯示器。倘若您有任何問題或需要產品介紹的話,請儘管和我聯絡。

謹上

王保羅
皇家液晶顯示器

III. 用 e-mail 回覆展開業務關係

✖ PLAY ALL | TRACK 055

To:	Paul Wang
Subject:	Re: Hello from Royal LCD

Dear Mr. Wang,

Thank you for bringing your company to our attention. We are interested in your offer of a product demonstration. As such, we would like to arrange a presentation. When would be a good time to schedule one?

Regards,

Greg Reynolds
Limitless Technologies

收件人：王保羅

主 旨：回覆：皇家液晶顯示器向您問候

王先生你好：

謝謝你告訴我們貴公司的一些事情。我們對於你所提議的產品展示感興趣。如上所言，我們希望可以安排一場簡報。安排在什麼時候會比較方便呢？

謹上

葛瑞格·雷諾茲
無限科技

IV. 電話展開業務關係必備句

介紹公司

A: **What does your company do?**

你們公司是做什麼的？

B: **We supply high-performance transistors to the international marketplace.**

我們供應高效能的電晶體給國際市場。

A: **What does your company produce?**

你公司是生產什麼的？

B: **My company produces solar modules for commercial application.**

我公司生產作為商業用途的太陽能模組。

銷售量

A: **What is your sales volume?**

你們銷售額是多少？

B: **Last year we sold more than 100,000 units.**

去年我們賣出超過十萬組。

> 回答也可以說 Our sales volume reached 100,000 units last year.

A: **How many units did you turn out last year?**

你們去年的產能表現如何？

B: **We shipped out over 50,000 units last year alone.**

光是去年我們的出貨量就超過五萬套。

....

公司優勢

A: **What else can you tell me about your company?**

關於你們公司還有什麼可以告訴我的嗎？

B: **You should also know that we provide a money-back guarantee.**

您應該也要知道我們提供退款保證。

....

期盼合作

A: **We would like to welcome you to sample our product.**

歡迎您試試我們的產品。

B: **We will definitely consider your offer.**

我們一定會考慮你的提議。

V. 用電話展開業務關係

Hank: Hello, is this Ms. Owen? This is Hank Lee from Global Industries.

Tanya: How can I help you, Mr. Lee?

Hank: I'm calling to introduce my company and our services. I think you'll be interested to hear what we have to offer.

Tanya: OK. What does your company do?

Hank: We produce hand-held power tools for the retail sector.

Tanya: I see. What else can you tell me?

Hank: You should know that all our products come with a money-back guarantee. Not only that, but we sold over 200,000 power drills just in the past two months.

Tanya: You don't say! You've sparked my interest, Mr. Lee. Why don't you leave your contact information with my secretary and we can schedule a product demonstration?

Hank: Excellent. I look forward to meeting you in person.

Tanya: As do I. I'll transfer you over now.

Hank: Thank you. Have a great day!

Tanya: You too. So long.

環球實業的李漢克打電話給一位潛在客戶。

您好,請問是歐文小姐嗎?這裡是環球實業的李漢克。

李先生,有什麼能效勞的嗎?

我來電是想要介紹敝公司以及我們的服務項目。我想您會有興趣聽聽我們的提議。

好吧。你們公司是做什麼的?

我們為零售商生產手持電動工具。

介紹公司

我瞭解了。還有其他可以告訴我的嗎?

您應該知道我們所有產品都有退款保證。不僅如此,光是過去兩個月我們就賣出超過二十萬支的電鑽。

公司優勢

銷售量

真的假的?李先生你引起我的興趣了。你不妨把聯絡資料留給我秘書,然後我們可以安排一場產品說明會。

太好了。我期待能見到您本人。

我也是,我現在就幫你轉過去。

謝謝。祝您有個美好的一天。

你也是。再見。

確認業務拜訪
Confirming a Business Meeting

I. 確認業務拜訪一定要會的句型

✖✖ PLAY ALL | TRACK 058

句型1 **拜訪提醒**

I just wanted to remind you of my upcoming visit to your company + 目的

- I just wanted to remind you of my upcoming visit to your company to introduce our company's latest products.

  我只是想要提醒你，我即將去你們公司拜訪並介紹我們公司的最新產品。

句型2 **確認時間地點**

To confirm, I am scheduled to meet with you + 時間、地點

- To confirm, I am scheduled to meet with you at 10 a.m. next Friday, December 30, at your office.

  確認一下，我預定在十二月三十日下星期五早上十點在你們辦公室和你見面。

句型3 設備需求

I would also appreciate it if you could + V.

- I would also appreciate it if you could arrange to have a screen and LCD projector in the conference room to facilitate my presentation.
  如蒙預先準備螢幕和液晶投影機以方便進行簡報的話，則不勝感激。

句型4 下次聯絡時間

I will contact you + 時間 + to reconfirm details.

- I will contact you in the next few days to reconfirm details.
  過幾天我再和你聯繫，再次確認細節。

II. 用 e-mail 確認業務拜訪

To: | Ken Burns

Subject: | Reminder: December 30 meeting

Dear Ken,

拜訪提醒 I just wanted to remind you of my upcoming visit to your company to introduce our company's latest products. **確認時間地點** To confirm, I am scheduled to meet with you at 10 a.m. next Friday, December 30, at your office.

Please note that I have already mailed you our company's most recent catalog, so you can preview any of these items before we meet.

設備需求 I would also appreciate it if you could arrange to have a screen and LCD projector in the conference room to facilitate my presentation. If that is not possible, please let me know, and I will bring my own portable equipment.

下次聯絡時間 I will contact you in the next few days to reconfirm details.

Thank you for your time. I look forward to meeting with you soon.

Kind regards,

Harry Wu, Sales Representative
Wisegrowth, Inc.
333-134-5676 ext. 146 (office)
445-786-3476 (cell)

———————— 中文翻譯 ————————

收件人：肯恩‧波恩斯

主 旨：提醒十二月三十日的會面

親愛的肯恩：

我只是想要提醒你，我即將到貴公司拜訪並介紹敝公司的最新產品。確認一下，我預定會在十二月三十日下個星期五早上十點在你們辦公室和你見面。

請留意我已將敝公司最新的型錄寄給你，所以在我們見面前你可以事先看一下這些商品。

如蒙預先準備會議室的螢幕和液晶投影機以方便進行簡報的話，則不勝感激。如果不可行，請讓我知道，我會把我的攜帶式設備帶去。

過幾天我再和你聯繫，再次確認細節。

感謝你撥出寶貴的時間。我期待盡快和你見面。

謹上

業務代表 吳哈利
明智發展公司
333-134-5676 分機 146（公司電話）
445-786-3476（手機）

Ⅲ. 用 e-mail 回覆業務拜訪

To:	Harry Wu
Subject:	Re: Reminder: December 30 meeting

Dear Harry,

Thanks for the reminder[1] about your upcoming visit to our company. I have received your catalog, and I look forward to learning more about your company's newest products. I will make sure that the items you've requested[2] are set up in the conference room <u>prior to</u> your arrival.

I will see you next Friday at 10 a.m.

> prior to 為介系詞片語，表示「在……之前」的意思，為正式的用法。

Sincerely,

Ken

收件人：吳哈利

主 旨：回覆：提醒十二月三十日的會面

親愛的哈利：

感謝你提醒即將來我們公司拜訪的事。我有收到你們的型錄，並且期待能更瞭解你們公司的最新產品。我會確認你所要求的這些配備在你到達之前會在會議室裡設置好。

下個星期五早上十點見。

謹上

肯恩

1. reminder [rɪˋmaɪndə] *n.* 作為提醒的人事物

2. request [rɪˋkwɛst] *v.* 請求；拜託

IV. 電話確認業務拜訪必備句

拜訪提醒

A: **Are we supposed to meet next week?**

我們下星期是不是應該要見面？

B: **Yes. We are scheduled to get together next week to review the changes to the contract.**

是的。我們預定下星期要一起再討論合約修改的地方。

....

確認時間跟地點

A: **I just wanted to confirm that we will be meeting at your company tomorrow morning at nine a.m.**

我只是要確認明天早上九點我們會在你公司見面。

B: **That's correct. Just give your name to the receptionist when you arrive.**

沒有錯。你到的時候只要告訴櫃臺人員你的名字就可以了。

A: **Is our meeting in two weeks still on?**

我們兩個星期後的會議還會進行嗎？

B: **Yes. We are scheduled to meet at my office at two o'clock, two weeks from now.**

會。我們預定兩個星期後兩點的時候在我辦公室見面。

設備需求

A: **I'd appreciate your arranging some presentation equipment for our meeting next week.**

如蒙預先準備我們下星期會議使用的簡報設備，則不勝感激。

B: **No problem. What exactly do you need?**

沒問題。你確切需要的是什麼？

A: **Would it be possible to have access to a projection screen at the presentation venue?**

簡報會場有沒有可能可以使用投影螢幕？

B: **I'm afraid that's not possible. We only have LCD monitors.**

恐怕不太可能。我們只有液晶螢幕。

下次聯絡時間

A: **I'll check in with you again next week to reconfirm the meeting.**

下星期我會再跟你聯繫，再次確認會面事宜。

B: **Great. Talk to you again soon.**

太好了。我們再聯絡。

Talk to you again soon. 為掛電話時的用語，表示「再聯絡」的意思，也可以說 Talk to you later。

V. 用電話確認業務拜訪

Sue: Hello. I'm calling for John Steele.

John: John speaking. How can I help you?

Sue: This is Sue Lin over at GeneTech. I'm calling about my visit to your company next week to introduce our latest products. I just wanted to make sure that it's still on.

John: Oh, that's right. When exactly are we meeting again?

Sue: We are scheduled to meet next Tuesday at 10:30 a.m. at your office.

John: Yes, I have it written down in my planner here. I'm looking forward to it.

Sue: Me too. And I'm certain that you will find our new products beneficial to your company.

John: Thanks for the reminder, Sue. I'll see you next Tuesday.

Sue: Great. By the way, I'd like to know if it would be possible to request some presentation equipment in the room where we'll be meeting.

John: No problem. Just e-mail me a list of what you need, and I'll make sure it's there.

Sue: That's great, John. Thank you. I'll call you again next week to firm things up.

基因科技公司的林蘇打電話給約翰·史蒂爾確認業務拜訪的時間。

你好。我要找約翰·史蒂爾。

我是約翰。我可以幫妳什麼？

我是基因科技公司的林蘇。我來電是關於下星期我要去貴公司介紹我們最新的產品。我只是要確定這事還在進行中。

拜訪提醒

喔，沒錯。我們下次見面的確切時間是什麼時候？

我們預定下星期二早上十點半在你辦公室見面。

確認時間
地點

好的，我記在行事計畫表上了。我很期待會面。

我也是。而且我確信你會發現我們產品對你們公司有幫助。

蘇，感謝妳的提醒，我們下星期二見。

太好了。對了，我想知道是否有可能在我們開會的房間要求一些簡報用的設備。

設備需求

沒問題。妳只要把需要清單寄給我，我會確認設備都安裝好。

那太棒了，約翰。謝謝。我下星期會再打電話把事情確定下來。

下次聯絡
時間

邀請蒞臨貿易展
Invitation to a Trade Show

I. 邀請蒞臨貿易展一定要會的句型

✖ PLAY ALL | TRACK 063

句型1 〉 **提出邀請**

Sb. is delighted to invite you to take a look at our booth + 時間 + 貿易展

- Ovid Book Publishers is delighted to invite you to take a look at our booth at next month's Asian International Book Fair.
  奧維德圖書出版公司很高興邀請你下個月到我們亞洲國際書展的攤位參觀。

....

句型2 〉 **展場活動**

You will have the chance to + V.

- You'll have the chance to get an exclusive look at our new digital education series.
  您將有機會獨家一窺我們的新數位教學系統。

句型3 展場位置

Our booth number is + 號碼, and we will be set up in + 位置

- Our booth number is 254, and we will be set up in the West Wing of Pavilion 2.

  我們的攤位編號是二五四，將設在展示館二館的西側。

....

句型4 參觀提醒

Don't forget + to V. for a chance + to V.

- Don't forget to print out the attached coupon and bring it to the show for a chance to win a free iPad.

  別忘了將隨附的優待券列印出來並帶到展場，就有機會免費獲得 iPad。

II. 用 e-mail 邀請蒞臨貿易展

PLAY ALL | TRACK 064

To: Joe Dickinson

Subject: Visit us at the Asian International Book Fair (AIBF): Jan. 16–18, 2016

Dear Joe,

展出邀請

Ovid Book Publishers is delighted to invite you to take a look at our booth at next month's Asian International Book Fair.

I will be managing the booth personally the entire day on all three days, so please drop by any time, and I would be happy to introduce our latest print products to you. I'm certain that your customers will be very interested in these new products.

展場活動

What's more, you'll have the chance to get an exclusive look at our new digital education series, which is due out on the market next February. So come join us and be one of the first to test-drive our revolutionary multimedia products.

展場位置

Our booth number is 254, and we will be set up in the West Wing of Pavilion 2. Just look for our company's signs and banners to find us.

參觀提醒

Lastly, don't forget to print out the attached coupon and bring it to the show for a chance to win a free iPad.

If you have any questions, please don't hesitate to contact me.

We look forward to seeing you at the AIBF.

Sincerely,

Melody Lin, Marketing Executive
Ovid Book Publishers

中文翻譯

收件人：喬‧迪金森
主　旨：謹於二〇一六年一月十六日至十八日蒞臨亞洲國際書展

親愛的喬：

奧維德圖書出版公司很高興邀請您下個月到我們亞洲國際書展的攤位參觀。

這三天我本人都會整天在攤位上負責處理展場事宜，所以隨時歡迎順道過來參觀，我會很樂於向您介紹我們最新的出版品。我確信您的顧客對我們這些新產品會很感興趣。

除此之外，您將有機會獨家一窺我們預計在明年二月上市的新數位教學系列。所以來加入我們，成為我們革命性多媒體產品的首批體驗者吧。

我們的攤位號碼是二五四，將設在展示館二館的西側。只要尋找我們公司的標誌和廣告橫幅就能找到我們。

最後，別忘了將隨附的優待卷列印出來並帶到展場，就有機會免費獲得 iPad。

如果您有任何問題的話，請別客氣儘管聯絡我。

我們期盼在亞洲國際書展見到您。

謹上

行銷經理　林美樂蒂
奧維德圖書出版公司

Ⅲ. 用 e-mail 回覆邀請

To: Melody Lin

Subject: Re: Visit us at the Asian International Book Fair (AIBF) : Jan. 16–18, 2016

Dear Melody,

Thank you for the invitation. I have noted your booth number and location at the AIBF, and I will be sure to <u>drop by.</u>

I am also very interested in trying out your new digital products, and seeing how they match up with the products offered in the U.S. If possible, please e-mail me an information and pricing catalog so that I can get a preview before coming to the show.

> drop by 表示「順道拜訪」，也可以用 drop in、come over、stop by、stop in 等動詞哦。

Well, it'll be a pleasure to see you at the show. I'll be sure to e-mail you if I have any questions.

Sincerely,

Joe

收件人：林美樂蒂

主　旨：回覆：謹於二○一六年一月十六日至十八日
　　　　蒞臨亞洲國際書展

親愛的美樂蒂：

感謝妳的邀請。我已經記下你們在亞洲國際書展的攤位號碼以及位置，我一定會過去參觀。

我也很有興趣試用一下你們新的數位產品，看看它們和美國所推出的產品是否並駕齊驅。如果可以的話，請把資料以及價目表用電子郵件寄給我，這樣我可以在去展場之前先預覽一下。

嗯，可以在展場上見到妳一定很棒。如果有任何問題的話我一定會用電子郵件跟妳聯絡。

謹上

喬

Ⅳ. 電話邀請蒞臨貿易展必備句

提出邀請

A: **I'd like to learn more about your company and its products.**

我想要知道更多關於你們公司以及產品的事。

B: **Then, please come and visit our booth at the trade show this week.**

那麼，請這個星期到我們貿易展的攤位來參觀。

展場活動

A: **Will you be giving a demo of your products at the trade show?**

你會在貿易展上介紹你的產品嗎？

B: **Yes. Our representatives will be demonstrating how to use our products.**

會的。我們的業務人員展示如何使用我們的產品。

A: **You'll have a chance to get a sneak preview at the latest version of our products.**

你將有機會先目睹我們產品的最新版本。

B: **Great to know. I'll definitely be there for that.**

很高興知道這件事。我一定會為此去的。

展場位置

A: **In which part of the convention center will your booth be?**

你們攤位在會議中心哪一區呢？

B: **We are in section A of Pavilion 3, with the rest of the multimedia companies.**

我們在展示三館的A區，和其他多媒體公司在一起。

A: **How can we find your booth?**

我們要怎麼找到你的攤位？

B: **Our booth number is 56B, and it's near the entrance of the hall.**

我們的攤位號碼是56B，靠近展覽館入口處。

....

參觀提醒

A: **Don't forget to present your coupon number at the booth to enter our <u>sweepstake.</u>**

別忘了在攤位上出示優惠券的號碼，以參加我們的抽獎。

> sweepstake 指一種抽獎活動，如果抽到你的名字就有機會贏得大獎項，也可用來指彩金獨得的一種比賽。

B: **I won't forget. And I do hope that it's a lucky number!**

我不會忘記的。我希望那是個幸運號碼！

V. 用電話邀請蒞臨貿易展

Donna: Hi. Is Greg Thompson in?

Greg: Yes, this is Greg. Is this Donna Kao?

Donna: It sure is. I'm just calling to remind you to stop by and visit us at our booth at the upcoming Taipei Trade Show this spring.

Greg: I'm already planning to do so. Any surprises this year?

Donna: Well, we will be introducing our latest line of energy-efficient devices at this year's event.

Greg: I've been wanting to get a closer look at those.

Donna: You can do so if you stop by booth 88 in section C of the trade complex. That's where you'll find us.

Greg: I'm writing down your booth number now.

Donna: I'll e-mail this information to you as well. And if you have any questions, just contact me at anytime.

Greg: Sounds great. I'm looking forward to seeing you soon.

高唐娜打電話邀請潛在客戶來參觀她們在貿易展的攤位。

嗨。葛瑞格‧湯普森在嗎？

是的，我就是葛瑞格。妳是高唐娜嗎？

沒錯。我只是打電話提醒你今年春天即將來臨的　提出邀請
台北貿易展你要順道過來我們攤位參觀。

我已經打算要去了。今年有什麼令人驚喜的嗎？

嗯，在今年的貿易展上我們會介紹最新系列的節　展場活動
能裝置。

我一直想要仔細看看這些裝置。

如果你到貿易大樓C區八十八號攤位來參觀的話　展場位置
就可以看到。你可以在那裡找到我們。

我現在把妳的攤位號碼寫下來。

我也會將這個資訊寄電子郵件給你。如果你有任
何問題的話，隨時打電話給我。

聽起來很棒。期待很快就可以見到妳。

I. 安排會面一定要會的句型

✖ PLAY ALL | TRACK 068

句型1〉 **訂房**

I have booked a room for you + at 地點 + for 一段時間

- I have booked a room for you at the Regal Inn for the length of your stay.

  你停留這段時間我已經幫你在富豪酒店訂了房間。

....

句型2〉 **行程安排**

I have come up with sth. for your visit.

- I have also come up with an itinerary for your visit.

  我也為你的造訪安排了一個行程。

句型3 溫馨提醒

Please note that S. + V. （氣候狀況、文化習慣）

- Please note that winter weather in Taipei can be cool and rainy.
  請留意台北冬天的天氣可能又濕又冷。

....

句型4 旅途愉快

Sb. wish you + 祝福

- We wish you a safe journey.
  祝你旅途平安。

II. 用 e-mail 安排會面

X PLAY ALL | TRACK 069

To: Ken Fields

Subject: Upcoming Meeting in Taiwan

Dear Ken,

I am writing to confirm the details of your upcoming visit to Taiwan from January 4 to January 7. I have booked a room for you at the Regal Inn for the length of your stay.

訂房

As per your request, I have also come up with an itinerary for your visit. I will be at the airport to pick you up when you arrive on the evening of January 4. For our scheduled meeting on January 5, I have arranged for a car to pick you up at the hotel and bring you to our office. Since it will be your first time in Taipei, I have also organized a day of sightseeing[1] for you on January 6. For further details, please refer to the attached[2] itinerary.

行程安排

溫馨提醒

Please note that winter weather in Taipei can be cool and rainy. Also, you may want to bring some casual clothes for the city tour that has been planned.

If you need any clarifications,[3] please don't hesitate to drop me a line.[4]

旁途愉快

We look forward to seeing you in Taipei and wish you a safe journey.

Regards,

Wes

中文翻譯

收件人：肯恩・菲爾茲
主　旨：即將在台灣見面

親愛的肯恩：

我寫信是要確認你將於一月四日至七日來台拜訪的細節。你停留這段時間我已經幫你在富豪酒店訂了房間。

根據你的要求，我也為你的造訪想了一個行程計畫。你一月四日晚上抵達時，我會到機場接你。關於我們預定一月五日的會面，我已經安排一部車去飯店接你到我們公司。由於這是你第一次來台北，我也替你規劃一月六日那天的一日觀光行程。關於其他更多的細節，請參閱附加檔案的行程表。

請留意台北冬天的天氣可能又濕又冷。此外，你可能會想要帶些休閒服，可以在所規劃的市區觀光行程中穿。

如果你需要任何說明，請不要客氣，儘管寫封短信給我。

我們期待在台北見到你，並祝你旅途平安。

謹上
維斯

1. **sightseeing** [ˋsaɪtˏsiɪŋ] *n.* 觀光

2. **attached** [əˋtætʃt] *adj.* 附加的

3. **clarification** [ˏklɛrəfəˋkeʃən] *n.* 說明；闡明

4. **drop sb. a line** *v. phr.* 寫封短信

Ⅲ. 用 e-mail 回覆會面安排

To: Wes Ko

Subject: Re: Upcoming Meeting in Taiwan

Dear Wes,

Thank you for confirming the dates and sending me the details of my upcoming visit to Taipei. I am very much looking forward to this visit.

If any questions come up, I'll be sure to let you know.

> if any questions come up 與 if you have any questions 意思相近，come up 表示「（問題、困難等）出現、發生」。

Thanks again for the information. I will see you in Taipei on January 4.

> 在約定見面的信函中，最後應該要再提到預定見面的日期或地點，其他說法像是：I look forward to seeing you in Taipei on January 4.

Sincerely,

Joe

收件人：柯維斯

主　旨：回覆：即將在台灣會面

親愛的維斯：

謝謝你確認日期，並寄給我即將到台北的行程細節。我非常期待這次的拜訪。

如果想到任何問題的話，我一定會讓你知道。

再次感謝這些資訊。一月四日我會在台北跟你見面。

謹上

喬

IV. 電話安排會面必備句

✗ PLAY ALL | TRACK 071

訂票與訂房

A: I just wanted to confirm that I have booked my airline tickets to visit your office this summer.

我只是要確認我已經訂好這個夏天去你公司拜訪的機票了。

B: That's great to hear. We'll look forward to seeing you then.

很高興聽到這個消息。我們期待屆時見到你。

A: I have made a reservation for you at the Chelsea Grand Hotel.

我已經在切爾西大飯店幫你預訂了房間。

B: Thanks. I appreciate your assistance.

謝謝。我很感謝你的協助。

行程安排

A: I will be in town for about three days.

我會在城裡待三天左右。

B: Great. I have organized a complete itinerary for your trip.

好的。我已經為你這次旅程規劃一個完整的行程。

溫馨提醒

A: Just a reminder that the summer weather here can be very hot and humid.

只是要提醒，這裡夏天的天氣可能會非常炎熱潮溼。

B: Thanks for the reminder. I'll be sure to bring the right clothes.

多謝提醒。我會帶些合適的衣服。

A: Please note that people here dress pretty conservatively.

請留意這裡的人穿著都相當保守。

B: That's good to know. Thanks.

我知道了。謝謝你。

旅途愉快

A: Have a safe flight and see you in Taipei.

祝你飛行平安，台北見囉。

B: Thanks. Looking forward to it.

謝謝。我很期待。

V. 用電話安排會面

Helen: Good morning. I'm calling for Jerry Smithers.

Jerry: Jerry here. What can I do for you?

Helen: Jerry, this is Helen Wu. I am just calling to confirm the specifics of your upcoming meeting with us here in Kaohsiung.

Jerry: Good thinking. I've been wanting to go over this with you.

Helen: Well, you're scheduled to be in Kaohsiung for five days. I have booked a suite for you at the Harbor Hotel.

Jerry: Great. I enjoyed my stay there last time.

Helen: According to our itinerary, we have meetings scheduled at our office for most of your visit. But your final day will be free for sightseeing.

Jerry: Good. What will the weather be like when I visit?

Helen: It should be a bit hot, I'm afraid.

Jerry: That's OK. I'm still looking forward to meeting with you in Kaohsiung soon.

海倫打電話給傑瑞確認他即將到高雄的行程安排及氣候等相關細節。

早安,我想找傑瑞·史密瑟斯。

我就是傑瑞。請問有什麼我可以效勞的地方?

傑瑞,我是吳海倫。我打來只是想確認你即將與我們在高雄會面的細節。

妳設想真是周到。我一直想和妳再確認這件事。

是這樣的,你預計在高雄待五天。我已經幫你在港口飯店訂好一間套房。

訂房

太好了。我上次住在那裡很喜歡。

根據我們的行程計畫,你來訪時大部分的時間都安排要在我們辦公室開會。不過最後一天可以自由觀光。

行程安排

好的。我去拜訪時天氣會怎麼樣?

恐怕會有點熱。

沒關係。我還是期待能快點與妳在高雄碰面。

取消會面
Canceling a Meeting

I. 取消會面一定要會的句型

✖ PLAY ALL | TRACK 073

句型1 **告知取消會面**

I regret to say + that S. + V.（取消會面）

- I regret to say that I must cancel my upcoming visit to Taiwan.

  很抱歉，我必須取消即將去台灣的參訪。

....

句型2 **説明原因**

Unfortunately, sth. has come up . . .

- Unfortunately, an urgent matter has come up here in my company.

  很遺憾，公司裡發生了緊急事件。

句型3 **希望改期**

I would like to reschedule my visit for + 時間

- I would like to reschedule my visit for this spring.

  我希望能夠將參訪改到春天的時候。

句型4 **補救方式**

If you would still like to discuss sth., perhaps we can arrange for + 補救方法

- If you would still like to discuss the matters we had scheduled, perhaps we can arrange for a teleconference via Skype.

  如果你仍想討論我們原定的事項,或許我們可以安排 Skype 視訊會議。

II. 用 e-mail 取消會面

To:	Wes Ko
Subject:	Cancellation of my upcoming meeting in Taipei

Dear Wes,

告知取消
會面

I regret[1] to say that I must cancel my upcoming visit to Taiwan. Unfortunately, an urgent matter has come up here in my company. This matter will require my full attention over the next weeks.

說明原因

希望改期

I would like to reschedule my visit for this spring. When I am more certain of my schedule, I will e-mail you some possible dates for a trip to Taiwan.

補救方式

If you would still like to discuss the matters we had scheduled, perhaps we can arrange for a teleconference[2] via Skype.

Once again, my apologies about this cancellation.[3]

Sincerely,

Ken

收件人：柯維斯

主　旨：取消即將於台北的會面

親愛的維斯：

很抱歉，我必須取消即將去台灣的參訪。很遺憾，公司裡發生了緊急事件，之後幾個禮拜我需要專心處理這件事。

我希望能夠將參訪改到春天的時候。等我時間較為確定後，我會再把可能去台灣的日期寄電子郵件給你。

如果你仍想討論我們原定的事項，或許我們可以安排 Skype 視訊會議。

對於取消會面，我再次致上歉意。

謹上

肯恩

1. regret [rɪˋgrɛt] *v.* 非常抱歉；遺憾

2. teleconference [ˋtɛlɪˌkɑnfərəns] *n.* 透過電視、電話進行的遠距會議

3. cancellation [ˌkænsəˋleʃən] *n.* 取消
（亦可拼成 cancelation）

Ⅲ. 用 e-mail 回覆會面取消

To: | Ken Fields

Subject: | Re: Cancellation of my upcoming meeting in Taipei

Dear Ken,

Thank you for your e-mail. I was sorry to hear that you have had to cancel your upcoming trip to Taiwan. However, I understand that you have urgent business to deal with[1] right now.

Once you know your schedule for the spring, we can work together to reschedule another time to meet here.

In the meantime,[2] we can continue to communicate by e-mail and phone.

Thank you once again for letting me know about this cancellation.

Sincerely,

Wes

收件人：肯恩‧菲爾茲

主 旨：回覆：取消即將於台北的會面

親愛的肯恩：

感謝你的來信。很遺憾聽到你必須取消即將來台之行。不過，我理解此刻你有緊急事務得處理。

一旦你知道今年春天的行程以後，我們可以一起重新安排其他見面的時間。

在這段時間內，我們可以透過電子郵件和電話繼續聯絡。

再次感謝你告知我這趟行程取消了。

謹上

維斯

1. deal with [dil] [wɪθ] *v.* 處理

2. in the meantime [ɪn] [ðə] [ˈmin͵taɪm] *phr.* 在這段時間

IV. 電話取消會面必備句

告知取消會面

A: I'm sorry, but I'm calling to let you know that I have to cancel our scheduled meeting.

很抱歉，我來電是要告訴你我必須取消預定的會議。

B: That's too bad. I hope everything is all right.

太遺憾了。希望你一切安好。

A: I just want to confirm that we are scheduled to meet on Monday.

我只是想確認我們有預定在星期一見面。

B: I apologize, but I am going to have to call off that meeting.

我很抱歉，我得取消這次的見面。

說明原因

A: We've had a crisis in our factory, and I need to stay here to take care of it.

我們工廠發生了危機，我得留在這裡處理。

B: I understand. Please let me know if there's anything I can do to help.

我瞭解。如果有任何我可以效勞的地方，請告訴我。

A: **Your e-mail mentioned that you need to cancel our meeting.**

你寄來的電子郵件提到你得取消我們見面的事。

B: **Yes. The workers in our factory are going on strike.**

沒錯，我們工廠的工人正在進行罷工。

....

希望改期

A: **Let's try to reschedule our meeting for sometime next week.**

我們試試看能否將會面改到下週某個時間。

B: **Sounds good. Let me know which dates will work best for you.**

聽起來不錯。再讓我知道哪天對你最方便。

....

補救方式

A: **If you have difficulty traveling, I could come to meet you at your office.**

如果你不方便來的話，我可以去你辦公室和你見面。

B: **That would be great. Let's set up a time.**

那太好了。我們訂個時間吧。

V. 用電話取消會面

Sam: Hi there. I'm just calling to speak with Louise Gu.

Louise: You've reached Louise.

Sam: Hi Louise. This is Sam Worthington. I'm very sorry, but I'm calling to cancel our upcoming meeting.

Louise: Oh, thanks for letting me know. Is everything OK?

Sam: Yes, I'm fine. Unfortunately, we've had a bit of a crisis in our office, and I need to be here to handle it.

Louise: I understand. If there's anything I can do to help, please let me know.

Sam: Thanks, but we have everything under control. I'd actually like to try to reschedule our meeting for sometime next month.

Louise: Sure. Just let me know what will work best for you.

Sam: Thanks. In the meantime, if you'd like to go through some numbers, we could Skype each other.

Louise: That could be a good idea. I'm still looking forward to meeting with you in person next month, though.

山姆因為公司出了一點狀況，必須打電話跟路薏絲取消預定的會面。

妳好，我想找顧路薏絲。

我就是路薏絲。

嗨，路薏絲。我是山姆·華斯頓。真的很抱歉，我來電是要取消我們近日即將見面一事。　　取消會面

噢，謝謝你告訴我。一切都還好吧？

是的，我還好。可惜我們公司出了點狀況，我得在這裡處理。　　說明原因

我瞭解。如果有任何需要我幫忙的地方，請告訴我。

謝謝，不過現在事情都在掌握之中。其實，我是想能否另外安排下個月找個時間來見面。　　希望改期

沒問題。只要告訴我你何時最方便就可以了。

謝謝。在這段期間，如果妳想跟我討論一些數目的話，我們可以用Skype聯絡。　　補救方式

那是個好點子。不過我仍然期待下個月能見到你本人。

感謝招待

Expressing Gratitude for Hospitality

I. 感謝招待一定要會的句型

✖ PLAY ALL | TRACK 078

句型1 表達此行愉快

. . . how much I enjoyed my recent trip to + 地點

- Just a brief note to let you know how much I enjoyed my recent trip to Taiwan.

  只是捎封短信讓你知道最近這趟台灣之旅讓我感到非常愉快。

....

句型2 感謝招待

It was nice of sb. + to V.

- It was nice of you to arrange a tour of the city for me.

  承蒙你為我安排城市旅遊，不勝感激。

句型3 〉 印象深刻的事

It was a real treat + to V.

- It was a real treat to visit the National Palace Museum.
  去參觀故宮博物院是一件非常棒的事。

....

句型4 〉 期待回報

On your next business trip to + 地點,
it would be my pleasure + to V.

- On your next business trip to Chicago, it would be my pleasure to take you around the city.
  下次你到芝加哥出差時，希望有榮幸能帶你四處參觀。

II. 用 e-mail 感謝招待

To: | Wes Ko
Subject: | Recent Meeting in Taiwan

Dear Wes,

表達此行愉快

Just a brief note to let you know how much I enjoyed my recent trip to Taiwan. It was very nice of you to arrange a tour of the city

感謝招待

for me, and <u>it was a real treat to</u> visit the National Palace Museum.

印象深刻的事

I was pleased that we were able to come to an agreement regarding exclusive agency. We certainly look forward to working with you in entering this new and exciting market.

On your next business trip to Chicago, it would be

期待回報

my pleasure to take you around the city.

Thank you once again for all of your assistance during my trip.

感謝函中除了表達謝意外，還可提到令你覺得愉快或有收穫的事情，其他説法如下：

- It was so exciting to see the National Museum.
- It was relaxing spending the entire day on the beach.
- What a treat it was / It was a real treat to see a performance at the Opera House.
- We especially enjoyed the day we spent shopping / seeing the historic monuments.

Sincerely,

Ken

───────── 中文翻譯 ─────────

收件人：柯維斯

主　旨：最近於台灣的會面

親愛的維斯：

只是捎封短信讓你知道最近這趟台灣之旅讓我感到非常愉快。承蒙你為我安排城市旅遊，不勝感激，並且去參觀故宮博物院是一件非常棒的事。

關於獨家代理一事，很高興我們能達成協議，我們真的非常期待與你們合作，進入這一塊生機蓬勃的市場。

下次你到芝加哥出差時，希望能有榮幸帶你四處參觀。

再次感謝你在我這趟旅程中所有的協助。

謹上

肯恩

Ⅲ. 用 e-mail 回覆感謝

To: Ken Fields

Subject: Re: Recent Meeting in Taiwan

Dear Ken,

Thank you for your e-mail.

It was my pleasure to be your host during your trip to Taiwan. I'm glad that we had the chance to meet and come to an agreement.

I also enjoyed spending time showing you the local sights.

I look forward to seeing you again soon. Please remember, you are always welcome to visit us here in Taiwan.

Thank you once again for your visit.

Sincerely,

Wes

收件人：肯恩·菲爾茲

主旨：回覆：最近於台灣的會面

親愛的肯恩：

謝謝你的來信。

在你來台期間能盡地主之誼是我的榮幸。我很高興我們有機會見面並達成協議。

帶你參觀本地景點的這段時間我也覺得很愉快。

期待能很快再與你見面。請記得，隨時都歡迎你到台灣來拜訪我們。

再次感謝你的到訪。

謹上

維斯

Ⅳ. 電話感謝招待必備句

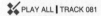 PLAY ALL | TRACK 081

表達此行愉快

A: **I'm just calling to let you know how much I enjoyed my recent business trip to Taiwan.**

我打來只是想告訴你我最近這次去台灣出差非常愉快。

B: **That's great to hear. We enjoyed having you.**

很高興聽到你這麼說。你來訪我們也很開心。

....

感謝招待

A: **Thank you for being such gracious hosts.**

謝謝你的盛情款待。

B: **It was our pleasure. I'm glad that everything worked out.**

這是我們的榮幸。我很開心一切都順利進行。

A: **I appreciate all of your assistance during my recent business trip.**

我非常感謝在我最近出差期間你所提供的所有協助。

B: **I'm glad that I could be of help.**

我很開心能幫上忙。

印象深刻的事

A: **Thank you again for taking me out for such a memorable dinner. The food was exceptional.**

再次感謝你帶我去吃令人難忘的晚餐，那裡的食物非常棒。

B: **That restaurant is famous for its food. I'm glad you liked it.**

那間餐廳的菜色非常有名，我很高興你喜歡。

....

期待回報

A: **You were such a great host. I look forward to the opportunity to reciprocate your hospitality.**

你真的是一個很棒的東道主，我期盼有機會能回報你的熱情款待。

B: **And I look forward to visiting you and your company soon.**

我也期待能很快去拜訪你和貴公司。

A: **Thanks for everything. It would be my pleasure to take you around the next time you visit St. Louis.**

感謝你所做的每一件事。下次你來聖路易斯時，希望我有這個榮幸帶你到處看看。

B: **Oh, that's not really necessary, but thanks.**

噢，不必這麼客氣，不過還是謝謝。

V. 用電話感謝招待

Eliza: Hello. I'm calling for George Hu.

George: Hello, this is George.

Eliza: Hi, George. This is Eliza Dobson. I'm just calling to let you know how much I enjoyed my recent business trip to Taiwan.

George: Oh, that's great to hear. It was a pleasure to have you visit.

Eliza: Well, you were a great host. Thanks for all your help in making my trip a success.

George: I'm glad that our negotiations went so smoothly.

Eliza: I think that's because we were able to meet face-to-face. I also enjoyed all of the great restaurants we went to.

George: We certainly had some memorable meals. I'm glad you enjoyed them.

Eliza: Well, on your next trip to America, I am going to return the favor.

George: Great. I look forward to it.

伊莉莎‧督柏森打電話給胡喬治，感謝他在她來台期間的招待。

哈囉，我想找胡喬治。

哈囉，我就是喬治。

嗨，喬治。我是伊莉莎‧督柏森。我打來只是要
讓你知道最近到台灣出差的旅程讓我覺得很開
心。

表達此行
愉快

噢，真高興聽到妳這樣說。妳能來訪是我們的榮
幸。

嗯，你真的是一個很棒的東道主。謝謝你所有的
協助，讓我此行圓滿成功。

感謝招待

我很開心我們的協商順利進行。

我想那是因為我們有機會面對面談。我也很喜歡
所有我們去的那些很棒的餐廳。

印象深刻
的事

我們確實吃了一些令人懷念的餐點。我很高興妳
喜歡。

那麼，你下次來美國時，我一定會回報你。

期待回報

太好了，我非常期待。

13 | 請求代理權
Request for Agency

I. 請求代理權一定要會的句型

✖ PLAY ALL | TRACK 083

句型1 > **請求代理權**

I am writing to express my interest in acquiring the rights of sth.

- I am writing to express my interest in acquiring the rights of exclusive agency in Taiwan for the distribution, promotion, and sales of Jacob & Marsh's gourmet products.

  我寫這封信是要表明對於取得雅各與馬爾斯精緻美食在台灣經銷、宣傳和販售方面獨家代理權的興趣。

句型2 > **說明公司優勢**

We have an influential presence in sth. （產業、市場）

- We also have an influential presence in the local food and wine community.

  我們在本地的食品及酒類市場亦佔有一席之地。

句型3 合作的好處

We will increase the presence of your brand here in + place

- Sage Enterprises will increase the presence of your brand here in Southeast Asia.
  賽吉企業將提升你們品牌在東南亞的知名度。

句型4 邀請進一步討論

To find out what benefits you can have by partnering with us, please contact us . . .

- To find out what benefits you can have by partnering with us, please contact us to set up a meeting to discuss this opportunity further.
  想瞭解與我方合作能帶給你們什麼樣的好處，請與我們聯絡，以安排會議進一步討論這個機會。

II. 用 e-mail 請求代理權

To:	corporate_relations@jacobmarsh.com
Subject:	Request for Exclusive Agency in Taiwan

Dear Sir/Madam,

請求代理權

I am writing to express my interest in acquiring the rights of exclusive agency in Taiwan for the distribution, promotion, and sales of Jacob & Marsh's gourmet products.

> 這裡的 acquiring 也可以換成 gaining 或是 being granted。

說明公司的優勢

We, at Sage Enterprises, are an established business organization with over twelve years of experience in gourmet food import and distribution. We also have an influential presence in the local food and wine community.

合作的好處

As you may be aware, Taiwan is an expanding market for gourmet food products. Sage Enterprises will not only increase the presence of your brand here in Southeast Asia, but we will also compile market research information to be used in making forecasts.

邀請進一步討論

To find out what benefits you can have by partnering with us, please contact us to set up a meeting to discuss this opportunity further.

In the meantime, please don't hesitate to call or write to me if you have any questions.

Yours truly,

Jo Hsiao, Director
Sage Enterprises

--- 中文翻譯 ---

收件人：corporate_relations@jacobmarsh.com

主旨：請求台灣獨家代理權

親愛的先生女士：

我寫這封信是要表明對於取得雅各與馬爾斯精緻美食在台灣經銷、宣傳和販售方面獨家代理權的興趣。

我們賽吉企業是擁有超過十二年食品進口、經銷經驗的老字號。我們在本地的食品及酒類市場亦佔有一席之地。

你可能會注意到，台灣是精緻美食產品擴張中的市場。賽吉企業不僅能提升你們品牌在東南亞的知名度，而且還能收集市場研究資訊來做預測。

想瞭解與我方合作能帶給你們什麼樣的好處，請與我們聯絡，以安排會議進一步討論這個機會。

這段時間，如果你有任何問題，請不要客氣，儘管打電話或寫信給我。

謹上

經理 蕭喬
賽吉企業

Ⅲ. 用 e-mail 回覆請求

To: | Jo Hsiao

Subject: | Re: Request for Exclusive Agency in Taiwan

Dear Ms. Hsiao,

Thank you for getting in touch with us, and for expressing your interest in acquiring exclusive agency from Jacob & Marsh for Southeast Asia.

We are indeed interested in your proposal. Over the past few years, our products have sold very well in Europe, and we are now evaluating[1] the prospect[2] of expanding our market presence into Southeast Asia. However, since you are requesting to act as our exclusive agent, I do need some time to formulate[3] the terms with my associates first. I will therefore get back to you again, once we have outlined[4] an agreement to discuss with you.

Thank you.

Kind regards,

John Smith
Marketing Executive
Jacob & Marsh, Co.

126, Abercrombie Road
Santa Monica, CA 90405

———————— 中文翻譯 ————————

收件人：蕭喬

主旨：回覆：請求台灣的獨家代理權

親愛的蕭小姐：

感謝妳與我們聯絡，也感謝妳對於取得雅各與馬爾斯在東南亞的獨家代理權有興趣。

我們確實對妳的提議感興趣。在過去幾年，我們的產品在歐洲銷售得非常好，現在我們正在評估將市場擴展到東南亞的可能性。然而，由於妳要求作為我們的獨家代理商，我需要一些時間先和合夥人制定條款。一旦我們將與妳討論的合約要點概述出來後，我會再與妳聯繫。

謝謝妳。

誠摯的祝福

約翰·史密斯
行銷經理
雅各與馬爾斯公司
90405 加州聖塔莫尼卡市
亞伯克隆比路一百二十六號

1. evaluate [ɪˋvæljəˏwet] *v.* 評估

2. prospect [ˋprɑˏspɛkt] *n.* （成功的）可能性

3. formulate [ˋfɔrmjəˏlet] *v.* 制訂

4. outline [ˋautˏlaɪn] *v.* 制定大綱

IV. 電話請求代理權必備句

請求代理權

A: **I'm calling to discuss the possibility of becoming your company's agent in Malaysia.**

我打電話是要討論成為你們公司馬來西亞代理商的可能性。

B: **I'm sorry, but we already have a sole agent in that region, so we cannot enter into business relations with another company.**

我很抱歉，我們那個地區已經有總代理商了，所以我們無法和其他公司建立業務關係。

A: **Have there been any developments regarding the possibility of exclusive agency?**

關於獨家代理的可能性有沒有任何進展？

B: **Yes. We are pleased to confirm the appointment of your company as our exclusive agent in the region we discussed.**

有的。我們很高興確認由你們公司來擔任我們所討論地區的獨家代理商。

說明公司優勢

A: **Our company has been in business for more than thirty years.**

我們公司從事買賣已經超過三十年了。

B: **This is one reason we've been looking to work with you.**

這是我們一直都想與你們合作的一個原因。

合作的好處

A: **With OPA, Co. as your exclusive agent, your company will be one of the biggest** <u>players</u> **on the Asian market.**

有OPA公司作為你們的獨家代理商，貴公司將成為亞洲市場最具主導地位的公司之一。

> player 在此指的是商場具有舉足輕重地位的公司。

B: **It is an exciting opportunity for us.**

對我們來說是個令人振奮的機會。

邀請進一步討論

A: **We invite you to visit us so we can further discuss this mutually beneficial business relationship.**

我們邀請你來拜訪我們，這樣我們才能進一步討論互惠的業務關係。

B: **Thank you. I will get back to you in the next few days.**

謝謝你。過幾天後我會跟你聯繫。

V. 用電話請求代理權

Karen: Hi. Is Fred Dobson there?

Fred: Yes, this is Fred. How may I help you?

Karen: This is Karen Lee from Lucky Trading Co. I'm calling to confirm your interest in granting us exclusive agency in Taiwan.

Fred: That's right. I sent you an e-mail about it last week.

Karen: Right. As you know, we are one of the most well-established trading firms in the leather goods sector in Taiwan.

Fred: Yes, I am aware of that, and I think that Taiwan may be a good market for our brand.

Karen: As your exclusive agent, we would certainly make your interests our very own.

Fred: That would certainly give us quite an advantage.

Karen: We would offer many other benefits to your company as well.

Fred: Well, Karen, I look forward to setting up a meeting with you to iron out the details of an agreement.

Karen: Wonderful. If you'd like, you could e-mail us a copy of the appointment letter and agency agreement to review first.

Fred: Sounds good. Talk to you soon.

凱倫打電話給弗萊德確認是否能擔任他們的獨家代理商，並約時間討論進
一步細節。

嗨。請問弗萊德‧督柏森在嗎？

是的，我就是弗萊德。有什麼可以為妳效勞的嗎？

我是幸運貿易公司的李凱倫。我來電是要確認你　　請求代理
是否有興趣允許我們成為台灣的獨家代理。　　　權

沒錯。上個星期我有寄信跟妳提到此事。

沒錯。如你所知，我們是台灣皮件業最有口碑的　　說明公司
貿易公司之一。　　　　　　　　　　　　　　　優勢

是的，我瞭解，也認為台灣對我們品牌來説可能
是不錯的市場。

身為你們的獨家代理商，我們絕對會將你們的利　　合作的
益視為自己的利益。　　　　　　　　　　　　　好處

那確實會帶給我們相當的好處 。

我們也會提供貴公司許多其他助益。

那麼，凱倫，我期待能和妳安排會面一起來討論
合約細節。

太棒了。如果你想的話，你可以用電子郵件將委
任函以及代理合約先寄給我們看看。

聽起來不錯。那儘快再跟妳聯絡。

請求著作權許可
Request for Copyright Permission

I. 請求著作權許可一定要會的句型

✖ PLAY ALL | TRACK 088

句型1 請求授權許可

I am writing to request permission to reprint sth.

- I am writing to request permission to reprint the following article in the March issue of our magazine Biz Buzz:

  我寫信是要請求允許下列的文章能在我們三月號的 Biz Buzz 雜誌上轉載：

....

句型2 是否付費

Please let me know if you would require + 費用

- Please let me know if you would require a <u>flat</u> licensing fee or royalties for permission to reprint.

  請讓我知道允許複印的話是否會收取固定的權利金或版稅。

  flat 在此表示「均一的；固定的」，與 fixed 意思相同

句型3 〉 標示所有權

Sb. will make sure to attribute the work correctly.

- I will, of course, make sure to attribute the work correctly.

  當然，我一定會確保這篇文章標示的所有權無誤。

句型4 〉 確認著作權所有人

If you do not control copyright to the requested material, . . .

- If you do not control copyright to the requested material, I would appreciate any information you can provide about whom I should contact.

  如果我們請求的內容你沒有著作權的話，若你能提供應該聯繫對象的資訊，我將感激不盡。

II. 用 e-mail 請求著作權許可

To:	Kelly Dobbs
Subject:	Request for Copyright Permission

Dear Ms. Dobbs,

請求授權許可

I am writing to request permission to reprint the following article in the March issue of our magazine *Biz Buzz:*

Author: Seth Myers

Title: Getting out of Debt Wisdom

Source: http://www.resource-management.com.nz/articles/12012011.htm

Biz Buzz, published by Rover Media, is a print journal with a monthly distribution of over 150,000 copies throughout Taiwan via newsstands and subscriptions. The magazine investigates current issues in business and asset management.

是否付費

Please let me know if you would require a flat licensing fee or royalties for permission to reprint. Any further details about payment are also welcome.

標示所有權

I will, of course, make sure to attribute the work correctly.

確認著作權所有人

If you do not control copyright to the requested material, I would appreciate any information you can provide about whom I should contact.

I look forward to hearing from you.

Regards,

Carl Zhang, Associate Editor
Biz Buzz

───────── 中文翻譯 ─────────

收件人：凱莉‧都伯斯

主旨：請求著作權許可

親愛的都伯斯小姐：

我寫信是要請求允許下列的文章能在我們《商場喧囂》三月號的雜誌上轉載：

作者：塞斯‧梅爾斯

標題：遠離債務的智慧

來源：http://www.resource-management.com.nz/
articles/12012011.htm

《商場喧囂》是由洛福媒體所出版，是一本每月在台灣透過書報攤及訂閱發行量超過十五萬份的平面出版期刊。本雜誌針對目前企業和資產管理方面的議題進行調查。

請讓我知道允許複印的話是否會收取固定的權利金或版稅。任何關於費用的進一步細節也歡迎妳說明。

當然，我一定會確保這篇文章標示的所有權無誤。

如果我們請求的內容妳沒有著作權的話，若妳能提供應該聯繫對象的資訊，我將感激不盡。

敬候佳音。

謹上

副編輯　張卡爾
《商場喧囂》

Ⅲ. 用 e-mail 回覆請求

To:	Carl Zhang
Subject:	Re: Request for Copyright Permission

Dear Mr. Zhang,

Thank you for your e-mail. We are delighted to learn that you would like to use one of our Web articles in your magazine. For one-time use, we normally charge a one-time flat fee of US$250. Please attribute the article to the author and cite the source where the article was originally published.

I have attached our standard copyright permission form. Please fill this out and return it to us at your earliest convenience.

Thank you again for your interest in our material.

Sincerely,

Kelly Dobbs,
Resource Management, Inc.

收件人：張卡爾

主旨：回覆：請求著作權許可

親愛的張先生：

感謝你的來信。我們很高興得知你們想在雜誌裡使用我們網站上的一篇文章。對於一次性的使用，我們通常收取單次兩百五十美元的固定費用。請將這篇文章的所有權標示為作者，並註明文章的原始出處。

我已附上我們的標準著作權許可表格。請將表格填好，在你方便時儘快回傳給我們。

再次感謝你對我們的資料感興趣。

謹上

凱莉‧都伯斯
資源管理公司

IV. 電話請求著作權許可必備句

✕ PLAY ALL | TRACK 091

請求授權許可

A: **I'm calling to request permission to use** some of your copyrighted material.

我打電話是想要請求允許使用受你們版權保護的資料。

B: **That's possible. What material do you want to use?**

那是可能的。你想要使用什麼資料?

A: **Have you had a chance to look at the content on our Web site?**

你有沒有機會看一下我們網站上的內容?

B: **Yes, and** we are interested in getting your permission **to use** some of it on our site.

有的,我們想要在網站上使用一些上面的內容,希望能得到你的允許。

是否付費

A: **Will we need to pay to use this content?**

我們使用這些內容需要付費嗎?

B: **Yes. We charge a flat licensing fee for use of our content.**

是的。使用我們的內容我們會收取固定的權利金。

標示所有權

A: **When you use this material, please remember to attribute it properly.**

當你使用這些資料時，請記得要正確標示其所有權。

B: **We'll be sure to do so.**

我們一定會照辦。

A: **Be sure to state our company's name as the owner of this material.**

務必將我們公司名稱標示為資料的所有人。

B: **I got it. We'll make certain that this gets done.**

我瞭解了。我們會確保做到。

....

確認著作權所有人

A: **Do you own the copyright to this material?**

你擁有這個資料的著作權嗎？

B: **Yes, I am the sole copyright owner.**

是的，我是著作權唯一所有人。

A: **I'm afraid we no longer hold the copyright to these articles.**

恐怕我們不再持有這些文章的著作權。

B: **Could you tell me whom I should contact to get reprint permission?**

你可以告訴我應該聯繫誰才能取得複印的許可嗎？

V. 用電話請求著作權許可

Alex: Hello. Alex Bai here. I'm calling for Sue Tripp.

Sue: This is Sue. What can I do for you?

Alex: I work in a small publishing company in Taiwan. I'm calling to request permission to use some of your copyrighted content.

Sue: Thank you for your interest in our work. What exactly do you want to use?

Alex: Specifically, we are interested in using the article "Career Changes at Middle Age" It appeared in your *Business Topics* magazine, and it was written by Don George.

Sue: That's a very popular article.

Alex: When it comes to payment, what are your standard terms?

Sue: We typically charge a flat fee for one-time use of our articles.

Alex: OK. And do you have any guidelines for attributing articles?

Sue: Just be sure to state the author's name and that the article was used with our permission.

艾力克斯打電話詢問轉載某篇文章的著作權許可。

你好。我是白艾力克斯。我想找蘇．崔普。

我是蘇。有什麼可以為你效勞的嗎？

我任職於台灣的一家小出版社。我來電是想請求允許使用一些受你們著作權保護的內容。

請求授權許可

感謝你對我們的著作感興趣。你們確切想用的是什麼內容？

具體來說，我們有興趣使用〈中年轉職〉這篇文章。它出現在你們《商務議題》雜誌中，是由唐．喬治所撰寫。

那篇文章很受歡迎。

談到費用，你們的收費標準條款為何？

是否付費

一次性的使用我們通常收取固定費用。

好的。文章所有權的歸屬你們有什麼要遵守的原則嗎？

只要確實標出作者姓名，及文章是經由我們允許使用即可。

標示所有權

介紹新業務關係
Introducing a New Business Relationship

I. 介紹新業務關係一定要會的句型

✖ PLAY ALL | TRACK 093

句型1 〉 介紹新業務關係

I am writing this brief e-mail to inform you of our company's new partnership with + 公司名稱

- I am writing this brief e-mail to inform you of our company's new partnership with AccuTech.

  我寫這封短信是要通知你我們公司和艾可科技新的合夥關係。

....

句型2 〉 未來的計畫

Our future plans include sth. (計畫)

- Our future plans include a complete merger of both companies.

  我們未來的計畫包括兩家公司完全合併。

句型3 〉 **帶來的好處**

S. will allow us + to V.

- This merger will allow us to increase our sales base and reduce our operating expenses.
  合併會讓我們增加銷售基礎並降低我們的營運費用。

....

句型4 〉 **對於貴公司的影響**

As far as our business with your company goes, . . .

- As far as our business with your company goes, this will remain unchanged.
  至於和你們公司之間的生意往來將維持不變。

II. 用 e-mail 介紹新業務關係

To: Guy Sayers

Subject: ABC Corp. teams up with AccuTech

Dear Guy,

介紹新業務關係

I am writing this brief e-mail to inform you of our company's new partnership with AccuTech. From January 1, we at ABC Corp. will be working as partners with AccuTech on a full-time basis.

未來的計畫

帶來的好處

Our future plans include a complete merger of both companies. This merger will allow us to increase our <u>sales base</u> and reduce our operating[1] expenses. The merger will also allow us to operate more efficiently.[2]

> sales base 譯成「銷售基礎」，base 是指構成某事主要部分的人、團體或金錢，如：customer base（消費者族群）、tax base（課稅基礎）、economic base（經濟基礎）。

對於貴公司的影響

As far as our business with your company goes, this will remain unchanged. However, please note that I will be moving to a new sales and marketing team. I will still be working with you and your company, though.

If you have any question about this new partnership, please feel free to contact me at anytime.

Sincerely,

Lili Chu, Senior Sales Executive
ABC Corp.

─────────── 中文翻譯 ───────────

收件人：蓋‧賽爾斯

主旨：ABC 公司和艾可科技展開合作

親愛的蓋：

我寫這封短信是要通知你我們公司和艾可科技新的合夥關係。從一月一日開始，我們 ABC 公司和艾可科技會以正式合夥關係合作。

我們未來的計畫包括兩家公司完全合併。合併會讓我們增加銷售基礎並降低我們的營運費用，也會讓我們在營運上更有效率。

至於和你們公司之間的生意往來將維持不變。然而，請留意我將調到新的業務行銷團隊去。不過還是會持續和你及貴公司合作。

如果你對於新的合夥關係有任何問題，請隨時與我聯繫。

謹上

資深業務主任　邱莉莉
ABC 公司

1. operating [ˈɑpəˌretɪŋ] *adj.* 營運的；運作的

2. efficiently [ɪˈfɪʃəntli] *adv.* 效率高；有效率地

Ⅲ. 用 e-mail 回覆新業務關係

To:	Lili Chu

Subject:	Re: ABC Corp. teams up with AccuTech

Dear Lili,

Thank you for informing me of the new partnership between your company and AccuTech. I was glad to hear that our business cooperation will remain unaffected.

<u>I will be sure to contact you if any questions should arise.</u>

Thank you again for the information.

Sincerely,

Guy Sayers, President
Project Fusion, LLC

本封 e-mail 用於感謝對方告知消息，因此一開始就先感謝對方，除了較禮貌外，也會讓收件人覺得愉快。此外，在結束信件前，也要再次感謝對方並加上禮貌語作為結束。如：I will be sure to contact you if any questions should arise 和 Thank you again for the information. 這兩句

收件人：邱莉莉

主旨：回覆：ABC 公司和艾可科技展開合作

親愛的莉莉：

感謝妳通知我貴公司與艾可科技之間新的合夥關係。我很高興得知我們的業務合作不受影響。

如果有任何問題的話，我一定會與妳聯繫。

感謝妳的資訊。

謹上

總經理　蓋‧賽爾斯
聯合企劃有限公司

IV. 電話介紹新業務關係必備句

告知新業務關係

A: **I'm just calling to let you know that we are forming a new partnership with Hills Co.**

我打電話是要告訴你我們將與希爾斯公司建立新的合夥關係。

B: **Congratulations, and thanks for the information.**

恭喜，也謝謝你的資訊。

··

未來的計畫

A: **We're going to cooperate with our new partner to enter the North American market.**

我們即將與新的夥伴合作進入北美市場。

B: **With this new partnership, expanding to the North American market shouldn't be a problem.**

有這個新的夥伴，要擴展北美市場應該不是問題。

A: **Because of the merger, we will consolidate our operations.**

因為合併的關係，我們將整頓營運。

B: **Please keep me informed of any major changes.**

任何重大變動請一定要通知我。

> keep me informed of sth 是表示「隨時讓我知道某事」的意思，為固定用法。

帶來的好處

A: **With this new partnership, we'll be able to offer you an even wider range of products.**

有了新的合夥關係，我們就能提供你範圍更廣的產品。

B: **Great. That will give us more choices.**

太好了。那我們就有更多的選擇了。

....

對於貴公司的影響

A: **Once the partnership is complete, I will be working in a new department.**

一旦合夥關係完成，我就會在新的部門上班。

B: **Please send me your new contact information, when you get a chance.**

你有空的時候請把新的聯絡資訊寄給我。

A: **After the new merger, our cooperation with you will continue as it always has in the past.**

新的合併之後，和你們的合作關係還是會和以前一樣持續下去。

B: **It's good to know that some things won't change.**

知道有些事情沒有改變是好的。

V. 用電話介紹新業務關係

Kevin: Hi. This is Kevin Lee. Is Rae Kelley there, please?

Rae: Rae speaking. How are you this morning, Kevin?

Kevin: Just fine. I'm just calling to let you know that our company will be forming a new partnership with Alpha Systems.

Rae: Is that right? Thanks for letting me know.

Kevin: This partnership will take place over the next few months.

Rae: Will there be any changes to the way we cooperate?

Kevin: Not at all. We'll still work together in the same way, though I will be moving to a new department.

Rae: Be sure to send me your new contact info.

Kevin: I will. This new partnership will make us more efficient, and we plan to pass these savings on to valuable customers like you.

Rae: That's always great to hear. Thanks again for the update.

李凱文打電話告知蕾‧凱立他們即將與艾爾發系統整合公司建立合夥關係。

嗨。我是李凱文。請問蕾‧凱立在嗎？

我就是蕾。凱文，今天早上好嗎？

還可以。我打電話只是要告訴妳我們公司即將和艾爾發系統整合公司建立新的合夥關係。 介紹新業務關係

是真的嗎？謝謝你讓我知道。

合夥關係會在這幾個月生效。

我們的合作模式會有任何改變嗎？

一點也不會。我們的合作方式還是一樣，不過我會到另一個部門去。 對於貴公司的影響

務必要將你新的聯絡資訊寄給我。

我會的。這次新的合作關係會讓我們更有效率，我們打算將省下來的花費回饋給像妳這樣的重要客戶。 帶來的好處

聽到這種事總是感覺很好。再次感謝你最新的消息。

貿易活動篇

本篇章中介紹貿易往來最常見的狀況,包括詢問產品、詢價、議價、下單、出貨、催款等貿易活動的流程,無論你是買方或賣方,我們提供你各種商務電子書信或電話英語的實用應對技巧。讓你在全球化的國際貿易中,輕鬆上手。

16 | 詢問產品
Product Inquiry

I. 詢問產品一定要會的句型

❌ PLAY ALL | TRACK 098

句型1 ▷ **說明如何取得聯絡**

I received your contact information from sb.

- I received your contact information from Christopher Holden, whom I believe you are familiar with.

  我從克里斯多福·荷登那裡取得你的聯絡資訊，我想你應該跟他很熟。

句型2 ▷ **對產品感興趣**

I am particularly impressed with sth. (商品名稱)

- I am particularly impressed with your Stack-and-Pack'em storage containers.

  我對你們的堆疊式收納箱印象特別深刻。

句型3 〉 提出顧慮

My only concern is sth.

- My only concern is <u>availability</u>.

  我唯一擔心的是有沒有現貨。

  availability 是指所要的物品可以取得或找到，在此用來表示有存貨可以使用的意思。

句型4 〉 索取資料

Could you please send me sth.?

- Could you please send me a comprehensive price list?

  你可以寄給我一份綜合價目表嗎？

II. 用 e-mail 詢問產品

To: | Yolinda Phelps

Subject: | Product Inquiry: Stack and Pack'em Containers

Dear Ms. Phelps,

My name is Alice Chen. I own a chain of stores in Taiwan called Delta Interiors.[1] We specialize in practical interior solutions.

說明如何取得聯絡

I received your contact information from Christopher Holden, whom I believe you are familiar with. He suggested I might be interested in one or more of your product lines and directed me to your Web site.

對產品感興趣

Having looked at your online catalog, I am particularly impressed with your Stack-and-Pack'em storage containers, and I expect

提出顧慮

they will sell well in all our outlets. My only concern is availability. We would like to begin with a large order (at least 1,500 units) of all sizes in blue, white and red. Do you have enough of those colors in stock? We need them to be delivered no later than March 15. Since your Web site did not list rates for your

索取資料

products, could you please send me a

> a chain of stores 是指「連鎖店」，亦稱為 chain stores，像超商、飯店等連鎖店就可稱為 supermarket chains、hotel chains。outlet 可稱為「銷售通路」或「暢貨中心」，為專賣過季或折扣商品的商店。

comprehensive[2] price list? If you have wholesale discounts available for large orders, please include a description with the price list. Thank you very much. I look forward to hearing back from you.

Sincerely,

Alice Chen
Delta Interiors

――――――― 中文翻譯 ―――――――

收件人：尤琳達‧菲爾普斯

主旨：產品詢問：堆疊式收納箱

親愛的菲爾普斯小姐：

我的名字是陳愛麗絲，在台灣擁有一家叫做三角室內裝潢的連鎖店。我們專門解決室內裝潢實際會遇到的問題。我從克里斯多福‧荷登那裡取得妳的聯絡資訊，我想妳應該跟他很熟。他認為我應該會對你們的一些產品系列有興趣，於是指引我到你們網站上看看。

看過你們的線上型錄之後，我對你們的堆疊式收納箱印象特別深刻，也預期它們在我們的銷售據點會賣得很好。我唯一擔心的是存貨問題。我們想要先從大筆訂單開始（至少一千五百組）包括藍的、白的、紅的各種尺寸。這些顏色你們有足夠的庫存嗎？這些商品需要在三月十五日前到貨。

由於網站上並未列出商品的價格，妳可以寄給我一份綜合價目表嗎？如果大筆訂單享有批發折扣價，請在價目表附上說明。感激不盡。敬候佳音。

謹上

陳愛麗絲
三角室內裝潢

1. interior [ɪnˋtɪrɪə] *n.* 室內 *adj.* 內部的

2. comprehensive [͵kɑmprɪˋhɛnsɪv] *adj.* 綜合的

Ⅲ. 用 e-mail 回覆詢問

To: Alice Chen

Subject: Re: Product Inquiry: Stack and Pack'em Containers

Dear Ms. Chen,

Thank you for expressing interest in our Stack-and-Pack'em storage containers. I'm happy to inform you that we do have plenty of the colors you requested in stock and available for purchase. However, in order to process your request we will need the address and telephone of your warehouse or distributor. In addition to the price list you asked for, I've also attached a purchase order which you will need to fill out to complete your order with us. Concerning your time constraints,[1] shipping to Taiwan should take no more than a week, so there shouldn't be any worries.

As for wholesale discounts, we are currently not offering any due to higher production costs. <u>But don't let that discourage you. We appreciate your business!</u> Prices fluctuate[2] and regular clients are offered discounted rates on a case-by-case basis.[3]

Regards,

Yolinda Phelps
Creative Plastics

> 不要害怕拒絕客戶的要求哦！不過在婉拒的同時別忘了感謝對方，以建立長久的合作關係。

收件人：陳愛麗絲

主旨：回覆：產品詢問：堆疊式收納箱

親愛的陳小姐：

感謝妳對我們的堆疊式收納箱感興趣。我很高興通知妳，妳需要的顏色我們還有許多現貨可供銷售。然而，為了處理妳的需求，我們需要妳倉庫或經銷商的地址及電話。除了妳所需要的價目表外，我也附上訂購單，妳必須填寫才算完成訂購。考量到你們的時限，貨運到台灣應該不會超過一個星期，所以應該不用太擔心。

至於批發折扣價，因為生產成本較高所以我們目前並沒有提供。但不要因此感到失望。我們很感謝此次的交易！價格會變動，並且會依狀況提供老客戶折扣價。

謹上

尤琳達・菲爾普斯
創意塑膠

1. constraint [kən`strent] *n.* 約束；限制

2. fluctuate [ˋflʌktʃəˏwet] *v.* 波動

3. on a case-by-case basis [ʌn] [ə] [kes] [baɪ] [kes] [besɪs]
   就個別的情況來看

IV. 電話詢問產品必備句

✘ PLAY ALL | TRACK 101

說明如何取得聯絡

A: I got your number from **Erica Wheldon,** whom I think you know.

我想你應該知道艾瑞卡‧威爾登，我從她那裡得知你的號碼。

B: Yes, we're very good friends.

是的，我們是很好的朋友。

對產品感興趣

A: **Which line of products were you interested in specifically?**

你有沒有特別對哪一系列的產品感興趣？

B: **I'm especially interested in the Roller-Derby Race Cars.**

我對Roller-Derby賽車系列尤其感興趣。

A: I would like know a little more about your **Roller-Derby Race Cars.**

我想要多知道一些關於你們Roller-Derby賽車系列的情報。

B: Sure thing. I'd be happy to answer any questions you may have.

沒問題。我很樂意回答你的任何問題。

提出疑慮

A: **My only concern is the delivery date. We need our order to arrive no later than the 21st of June.**

我唯一擔心的是交貨日。我們訂的貨必須在六月二十一日之前抵達。

B: **I think we can handle that.**

我想我們可以處理。

....

索取資料

A: **Could you send me the pricing information for those items?**

你可以寄給我那些商品的價格資訊嗎？

B: **Certainly. I'll get them out to you as soon as possible.**

當然。我會儘快寄給你。

> 通常產品相關的文宣品包括：手冊
> （brochure, pamphlet, booklet）、
> 型錄（catalog）、傳單（flier, leaflet,
> handout, circular）

V. 用電話詢問產品

Tina: Hello? May I speak with Mr. Wesley Cantor, please?

Wesley: Speaking. Who may I ask is calling?

Tina: My name is Tina Sanders from Trinity Kitchens. I was given your number by Shelly Thompson. She's a client of yours.

Wesley: That's right. What can I do for you Ms. Sanders?

Tina: Well, she tells me that you have the lowest prices on No-Scratch pots and pans in the county, and I was wondering which models you carry.

Wesley: I see. If you like, I could send you some literature on the models we have in that product line.

Tina: That would be great. Oh, one more thing before I forget: Can you send me the pricing information for your products as well?

Wesley: You bet. Why don't you give me your address, and I can get all that out to you this afternoon.

Tina: Great. Thanks a lot.

三合一廚具的蒂娜致電給廚具供應商代表衛斯里，詢問產品的相關訊息。

你好？我可以和衛斯里‧康德說話嗎，麻煩你了。

我就是。請問是哪位？

我是三合一廚具的蒂娜‧山德斯。我從雪莉‧湯普森那裡得知你的電話。她是你的客戶。　　説明如何取得聯絡

是的。山德斯小姐，有什麼可以為妳效勞的嗎？

嗯，她跟我說你們有全都最低價的防刮鍋具組，我想知道你們有哪些款式。　　對產品感興趣

我瞭解了。如果妳想要的話，我可以給妳一些那個產品系列款式的文宣。

那太好了。喔，在我忘記前還有一件事：你可以同時寄給我一份你們的產品價目表嗎？　　索取資料

當然。還是妳給我地址，我今天下午將全部的資料寄給妳。

太好了。非常感謝。

I. 詢價一定要會的句型

✖ PLAY ALL | TRACK 103

句型1 **考慮下單**

We're currently considering placing an order for sth.

- We're currently considering placing an order for your Super Soft Travel Pillows.
  我們目前正在考慮向你們訂購超柔軟旅行用枕。

....

句型2 **能否提供折扣**

Is there any way we could + V.?

- Is there any way we could negotiate a discount?
  有沒有商議折扣的可能呢?

句型3 提出疑問

We would like to know sth.

- In particular, we would like to know how defective merchandise will be dealt with.

  尤其，我們想知道瑕疵品會怎麼處理。

II. 用 e-mail 詢價

To:	Nick Fuller
Subject:	Travel Pillow Inquiry

Dear Mr. Fuller:

考慮下單　We're currently considering placing an order for your Super Soft Travel Pillows. I have looked at the prices listed on your 能否提供折扣　Web site. Is there any way we could negotiate a discount?

There is one other concern as well. What assurances[1] can you provide against defects?[2] Quality assurance is a big 提出疑問　concern of ours. In particular, we would like to know how defective merchandise will be dealt with. Will you provide a refund or will they need to be returned and replaced? In such cases, who will pay for return shipping costs?

Sincerely,

Pamela Hsu
Friendly Flyers

―――――― 中文翻譯 ――――――

收件人：尼克‧富勒

主旨：詢問旅行用枕

親愛的富勒先生：

我們目前正在考慮向你們訂購超柔軟旅行用枕。我已經看過你們網站上所列的價格。有沒有商議折扣的可能呢？

此外還有另一項顧慮。針對瑕疵品，你們能提供怎樣擔保呢？品質保證是我們很重視的問題。尤其，我們想知道瑕疵品會怎麼處理。你們會提供退款，還是商品必須退回更換？如果是這種情形，誰需要負擔退貨的運費呢？

謹上

徐潘蜜拉
友善飛行

1. assurance [əˋʃurəns] *n.* 保證；擔保

2. defect [ˋdiˌfɛkt] *n.* 瑕疵

III. 用 e-mail 回覆詢價

To: | Pamela Hsu

Subject: | Re: Travel Pillow Inquiry

Dear Ms. Hsu,

We are pleased that you are considering making an order for our Super Soft Travel Pillows.

Quality assurance is a concern we share. Rest Easy maintains[1] a defect-free policy. We guarantee complete refunds for defective merchandise. That means there is no need for returns or subsequent[2] worries about shipping costs. Most, if not all, defective merchandise is typically caught by our own QA team. We are confident you and your customers will be satisfied with the finished product.

As far as a discount is concerned, we are willing to negotiate. How large of an order were you considering? The larger the order, the greater the discount we'd be willing to offer.

Sincerely,

Nick Fuller
Rest Easy

收件人：徐潘蜜拉

主旨：回覆：詢問旅行用枕

親愛的徐小姐：

我們很高興妳正考慮訂購我們的超柔軟旅行用枕。

品質保證是我們共同關切的事情。高枕無憂一向維持無瑕疵政策。針對瑕疵商品，我們保證全額退費。也就是說，不需要退回商品或擔心後續的運費問題。就算不是全部，大部分的瑕疵品通常都會被我們的品管人員揪出來。我們有信心貴公司及你們的客人對成品會非常滿意。

說到折扣，我們願意商議。你們考慮的訂單量有多大呢？訂單量越多，我們願意提供的折扣就越多。

謹上

尼克·富勒
高枕無憂

1. maintain [menˋten] *v.* 維持

2. subsequent [ˋsʌbsɪkwənt] *adj.* 接下來的；繼之而起的

Ⅳ. 電話詢價必備句

考慮下單

A: **You've reached Alpine Apparels. This is Cathy speaking. How may I help you?**

你所接通的是山岳服飾。我是凱西，有什麼可以為你服務的嗎？

B: **Hello Cathy.** We're interested in placing an order for **the Polar Fleece jackets.**

哈囉，凱西。我們有興趣向你們訂購極地絨毛夾克。

能否提供折扣

A: Is there any way you could lower the price **if we increased our order?**

如果我們增加訂單，你們有沒有可能降價呢？

B: That depends. How many units are you willing to commit to?

視情況而定。你們願意承諾買多少組呢？

提出疑問

A: **What kind of quality assurance standards** do you have?

你們有什麼樣的品質保證標準呢？

B: **All of our merchandise is inspected and tested before leaving the factory.**

我們所有的商品在出廠前，都會經過檢查和測試。

A: **What do you need to know exactly?**

你還需要知道哪些確切的事呢？

B: **We need to know precisely when the order will be delivered.**

我們需要知道訂單送達的確切時間。

A: **We are curious as to the exact shipment date.**

我們想知道確切的出貨日期。

B: **Let me look that up for you.**

我來幫你查一下。

A: **Do you have any other questions?**

你還有任何其他問題嗎？

B: **Yes,** we would like to find out **the exact size of the shipping container.**

有，我們想要知道貨櫃確切的尺寸大小。

V. 用電話詢價

Vera: Hello. This is Vera Johnson.

Mike: Hi, Vera. This is Mike over at Timely Time Pieces. We're looking at putting in an order for some of your Rise and Shine alarm clocks.

Vera: Oh, the new Rise and Shine model. We have those in stock. How many did you want?

Mike: Well, we were hoping you could cut a little off the top if we placed a large order.

Vera: We could do that. Place an order of 5,000 units, and you'll get a 15% discount. How does that sound?

Mike: It sounds great, but I'll still have to talk to my people about it.

Vera: Of course. Was there anything else you needed?

Mike: Actually, yes. We'd like to know how many decibels the alarm sounds at.

Vera: I don't have that information on hand. Can I get back to you on that?

Mike: Naturally. I know it's something of a strange question.

Vera: I'll find out and get back to you soon.

Mike: That's great. I really appreciate it.

及時鐘錶零件行的麥克打電話給薇拉詢問商品訂購及價錢。

哈囉,我是薇拉·強森。

嗨,薇拉。我是及時鐘錶零件行打來的麥克。我們正在考慮訂購你們的起床閃耀鬧鐘。

考慮下單

喔,那款新的起床閃耀鬧鐘。我們目前有存貨。你要多少?

嗯,如果我們下的單量大的話,希望價錢上可以砍一點。

能否提供折扣

我們做得到。訂購五千件的話打八五折。聽起來如何?

聽起來很棒,但我還是得跟我們其他人談一下。

當然。還需要什麼嗎?

事實上,有的。我們想知道鬧鐘的分貝是多少。

提出疑問

目前我手邊沒有那項資料。我可以之後回覆你嗎?

當然,我知道這個問題有點怪。

我會找出來然後儘快回覆你。

那太好了。真的很感激。

報價後續追蹤
Price Quote Follow-up

I. 報價後續追蹤一定要會的句型

✖ PLAY ALL | TRACK 108

句型1 > **等待確認**

We are still awaiting sth.

- We are still awaiting your confirmation.
  我們還在等妳的確認。

句型2 > **推銷產品**

There isn't a more adj. + 商品 + available.

- There isn't a more popular or more comfortable pillow available.
  你找不到更受歡迎或更舒適的枕頭了。

句型3 〉 **給予協助**

If ..., we would be pleased to assist you in any way.

- If there is anything we can do to facilitate your order, we would be pleased to assist you in any way.

  如果在訂單上面有任何可以幫忙的地方，我們會很樂意提供協助。

句型4 〉 **期待合作**

We look forward to hearing back from sb.

- We look forward to hearing back from you soon.

  我們期待儘快聽到妳的回覆。

II. 用 e-mail 做報價後續追蹤

To: Pamela Hsu

Subject: Quotation Follow-up

Hello again, Ms. Hsu,

I'm writing again to follow-up on the previous quotation we sent you for the Travel Pillows you inquired about. I've attached the document to this e-mail, but there is a quick summary of our offer:

Item: Super Soft Travel Pillows　**Qty:** 5,000
Total Price: US$6,000.00　**Discount:** 10%

I originally sent this quotation to you on January 17. Perhaps you didn't receive it.

等待確認 We are still awaiting your confirmation. We are very eager to know if you would like to proceed with[1] the order. If the terms are acceptable, please let us know and we will ship it out to you immediately.

As you probably know, our Super Soft Travel Pillows are the top-selling travel

推銷產品 pillow on the market. There isn't a more popular or more comfortable pillow available. You will have trouble keeping this item on your shelves.

> can't keep this item on your shelves 字面意思是「商品無法在架上留太久」，即表示「熱銷」的意思。

We appreciate your business. If there is anything we can do to facilitate[2] your order, we would be pleased to assist you in any way.

We look forward to hearing back from you soon.

Sincerely,

Nick Fuller
Rest Easy

予協助

待合作

中文翻譯

收件人：徐潘蜜拉

主旨：報價後續追蹤

再次向妳問候，徐小姐：

我再次寫信是要追蹤上次在妳詢問後寄出的旅行用枕的報價。我把檔案附在信件中，不過我在這裡快速列出我們報價的摘要：

品項：超柔軟旅行用枕　　數量：五千
總價：六千美元　　　　　折扣：九折

原本我在一月十七日將這份報價寄給妳。可能妳沒有收到。我們還在等妳的確認。我們很想知道妳是否還想繼續這份訂單。如果這些條件能接受的話，請通知我們，我們將立即出貨給妳。

妳可能知道，我們的超柔軟旅行用枕是市面上最暢銷的旅行用枕。妳找不到更受歡迎或更舒適的枕頭了。這件商品將會熱銷，不會佔架太久的。

我們很感激這筆生意。如果在訂單方面有任何可以幫忙的地方，我們會很樂意提供協助。

我們期待儘快聽到妳的回覆。

謹上

尼克‧富勒
高枕無憂

1. proceed with [pro`sid] [wɪθ] v. 繼續進行

2. facilitate [fə`sɪləˌtet] v. 幫助；促進

Ⅲ. 用 e-mail 回覆追蹤

To: | Nick Fuller

Subject: | Re: Quotation Follow-up

Dear Mr. Fuller

Please accept my apologies for not getting back to you sooner. Our offices <u>have been closed</u> for the extended[1] Chinese New Year holiday. As such, we did not receive your e-mail in time to reply meaningfully. We are still thinking over your offer. Perhaps we can discuss the details over the phone tomorrow? We would like to seal[2] the deal as soon as possible.

Sincerely,

Pamela Hsu
Friendly Flyers

> 利用被動語態 have been closed 可避免將錯誤明確歸咎在某人或某事上，表示較客觀的原因。

收件人：尼克・富勒

主旨：回覆：報價後續追蹤

富勒先生你好：

很抱歉沒有儘快回信給你，請接受我的道歉。我們因為中國新年連假而沒有上班。因此，我們沒有及時收到你的來信並做有意義的回覆。我們還在考慮你的開價。或許我們可以明天在電話上談？我們想要儘早達成協議。

謹上

徐潘蜜拉
友善飛行

1. **extended** [ɪk`stɛndəd] *adj.* 延長的；擴張的

2. **seal** [sil] *v.* 確認；保證（契約、交易）

IV. 電話做後續追蹤必備句

等待確認

A: We were wondering if you still wanted to go ahead with the order.

我們想知道這份訂單是不是還要繼續處理呢？

B: **We do. Sorry about the delay.**

要的。很抱歉耽擱了。

A: We haven't heard back from you in a while.

我們有一陣子沒收到您的消息了。

B: **I'm really sorry about that. We've been really busy here lately.**

我真的很抱歉。我們這邊最近真的很忙。

A: **I'm sorry I couldn't call you back sooner.**

抱歉我沒有儘快回電給你。

B: **That's OK.** We're just waiting for your confirmation.

沒關係。我們只是在等你確認。

推銷產品

A: **I don't know if you were <u>having any second</u> thoughts, but you won't find a better model on the market.**

我不知道是否你有其他想法，不過你在市面上找不到更好的款式了。

> 對原本決定的事情有了其他想法可用
> have second thoughts about sth. 來表示。

B: **That's true. It is the best product out there. / Well, I'm not so sure about that.**

沒錯，這的確是最好的產品。／嗯，對此我不是很確定。

給予協助

A: **We'll be happy to help you with any questions you might have about your order.**

你在訂單上有任何疑問我們都很樂意為你解決。

B: **Actually, I do have a few things I'd like to ask you about.**

事實上，我的確有一些事情想要問你。

V. 用電話做報價後續追蹤

Tammy:	You've reached the Hat House. This is Tammy Tanner. How can I help you?
Chuck:	Hi, Tammy. It's Chuck from Henderson's Hats.
Tammy:	Hello, Chuck. I've been meaning to get back to you. We've had a bit of a busy week. Sorry about that.
Chuck:	It's OK. I know you said you needed that order we talked about, but we haven't gotten a confirmation yet. Should I ship it out?
Tammy:	Here's the thing. We're having second thoughts about the new hats. We're not sure they're going to sell well.
Chuck:	You should give them a chance, Tammy. There isn't a more comfortable winter hat out there.
Tammy:	I'm sure they're comfortable. What concerns me is how many I can sell.
Chuck:	I'm sure we can work something out.
Tammy:	Sorry to interrupt you, Chuck. I've got another call coming in.
Chuck:	That's fine. We can finish this later. Bye, now.
Tammy:	Thanks a lot. Bye, Chuck.

帽子供應商查克打電話給泰咪做報價後追蹤，並再次強調產品優勢。

您撥的是帽子之家。我是泰咪·唐納。有什麼能幫忙的嗎？

嗨，泰咪。我是漢德森帽子的查克。

你好，查克。我一直想回電給你。我們這週有點忙。很抱歉。

沒關係。我知道妳說妳要那份之前談過的訂單，但我們還沒得到任何確認。我該出貨嗎？　　等待確認

重點在這裡。我們對於這些新帽子有不同的看法。我們不確定它們會不會賣得好。

妳該試試看，泰咪。冬天的帽子妳在外面找不到更舒適的了。　　推銷產品

我確定它們很舒適。我擔心的是我可以賣掉多少。

我相信我們有解決辦法。　　期待合作

查克抱歉打斷你。我有另一通電話進來。

沒關係。我們可以晚一點再談。先說再見。

非常謝謝你。再見，查克。

I. 議價一定要會的句型

✖ PLAY ALL | TRACK 113

句型1 〉 **超出預算**

Unfortunately, sth. does not allow us to meet the quoted price.

- Unfortunately, our budget does not allow us to meet the quoted price.

  很可惜，我們的預算不容許我們接受這份報價。

....

句型2 〉 **狀況說明**

At the current rate, we would have to + V.

- At the current rate, we would have to lower our order from 4,000 to 3,000 units.

  以目前價格來看，我們必須將訂單從四千降到三千組。

句型3〉 **議價**

Is there any way we could + V.?

- Is there any way we could get 4,000 units for $60,000?

  我們有辦法用六萬元買四千組嗎？

....

句型4〉 **期待達成交易**

We would like to come to a deal . . .

- We would like to come to a deal as soon as possible.

  我們希望能儘早達成交易。

II. 用 e-mail 議價

To: Paul Rogers

Subject: Over Our Budget

Greetings Mr. Rogers,

Thank you for your prompt reply. I wasn't expecting to hear back from you so quickly.

超出預算

Unfortunately, **our budget** does not allow us to meet the quoted price. Due to other

狀況說明

investments, our funds are limited. At the current rate, we would have to **lower our order from 4,000 to 3,000 units.** Since this number is a bit too small for our needs,

議價

we are forced to ask for a discount. Is there any way we could **get 4,000 units for $60,000?**

In our past dealings you have known us to be very straightforward.[1] We also appreciate your willingness to accommodate[2] our needs. <u>This is why we come back to do business with your company.</u>

We are in somewhat of a hurry to receive the units, so we would like to come to a deal as soon as possible. Thank you again.

期待達成
交易

> 議價時可表示與對方一直以來都合作愉快，並希望能再次合作，作為議價談判的籌碼。

242

Sincerely,

Wendy Lin, Area Manager
Dragon Distributors

———————— 中文翻譯 ————————

收件人：保羅‧羅傑斯

主旨：超出預算

羅傑斯先生你好：

感謝你迅速回覆。我沒有想到你這麼快就回覆了。很可惜，我們的預算不容許我們接受這份報價。因為還有其他投資，我們的資金有限。以目前價格來看，我們必須將訂單從四千組降到三千組。由於這個數量和我們的需求比起來又太少，因此我們被迫要求折扣。我們有辦法用六萬元買四千組嗎？

從我們過去的交易，你必然知道我們是非常直率的。我們也很感激你們願意配合我們的需求。那也是為什麼我們一再和你們做生意的原因。

我們有點急需收到這些商品，所以希望能儘早達成交易。再次感謝你。

謹上

區經理　林溫蒂
龍牌經銷商

1. straightforward [ˌstretˋfɔrwəd] *adj.* 直接坦率的

2. accommodate [əˋkɑməˌdet] *v.* 配合；舒適

Ⅲ. 用 e-mail 回覆議價

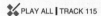

To:	Wendy Lin
Subject:	Re: Over Our Budget

Dear Ms. Lin,

We understand your budget[1] and time constraints. For the number you mentioned, the best we can offer is 3,500 units. Your business is important to us, so we are willing to offer a onetime[2] discount. If you really need 4,000 units, then our price will be $68,000. Is either of these terms acceptable?

Sincerely,

Paul Rogers, Sales Associate
Digital Deals

收件人：林溫蒂

主旨：回覆：超出預算

親愛的林小姐：

我們能理解妳的預算及時間限制。妳所提到的數字，我們最多只能提供三千五百組。你們的生意對我們來說很重要，所以我們願意提供一次性折扣。如果你們真的需要四千組，那我們的價錢會是六萬八千元。這兩個條件哪個可以接受呢？

謹上

銷售助理　保羅·羅傑斯
數位買賣

1. budget [`bʌdʒət] *n.* 預算

2. onetime [`wʌn`taɪm] *adj.* 一次性的

Ⅳ. 電話議價必備句

✖ PLAY ALL | TRACK 116

超出預算

A: The price you quoted is a
little out of our budget.

你報的價有點超出
我們的預算。

B: What did you have in mind?

你預期的價格是多
少？

狀況說明

A: Without a discount, we
will be forced to lower our
order.

沒有折扣的話，我
們得被迫刪減訂
量。

B: I'm sorry to hear that, but I'm
afraid we can't go any lower
on the price.

我很遺憾聽到你這
麼說，但恐怕我們
價格無法再降了。

議價

A: Would it be possible to
order 3,000 units at 500,000
NTD?

可不可能以新台幣
五十萬訂購三千組
呢？

B: At that price, the best thing
we can offer is 2,500 units.

以那個價錢，我
們最多能提供兩
千五百組。

A: **I can't tell you how much we would appreciate a discount.**　　有折扣的話我們將會無比的感激。

B: **Well, how big of a discount were you thinking of?**　　嗯，你們想要多少折扣？

A: **Could you lower the price a bit?**　　你可以把價錢再降一點嗎？

B: **Unfortunately not. That is our final offer.**　　很遺憾不行。那是我們的底價了。

....

期待達成交易

A: We are very eager to come to a deal as soon as possible.　　我們非常希望能儘早達成交易。

B: I understand. I'll get back to you within the hour. How does that sound?　　我瞭解。我會在一小時內回覆你。你覺得如何？

V. 用電話議價

Wes: Hello, Hope. Wes here.

Hope: Hi, Wes. I'm glad you called. What did you think of our offer?

Wes: Actually, it's a bit higher than we were hoping. Frankly, it's just out of our budget.

Hope: That's too bad. How much were you thinking of spending on the order?

Wes: We're prepared to pay as much as $150,000, but that's really the highest we can go. Could you offer us a discount?

Hope: Hmm. I'll have to get back to you on this. I need to do some calculations.

Wes: Alright. When do you think you could give us an answer? We're very eager to come to an agreement as soon as possible.

Hope: Would tomorrow morning be soon enough?

Wes: That would be fine.

Hope: OK, then. I'll have a chat with my people, and give you a call first thing tomorrow.

Wes: Thanks a bunch, Hope.

供應商維斯打電話詢問顧客荷璞對開價是否滿意，荷璞表示超出預算並希望能給個折扣。

妳好，荷璞。我是維斯。

嗨，維斯。很高興你打來。你覺得我們開的價如何？

事實上，比我們希望的高了點。坦白說，超出我們的預算了。

那太糟了。你們預計要花多少錢在這筆訂單上？

我們打算最多十五萬元，但那是我們能出的最高價。妳可以提供我們折扣嗎？

嗯。我必須回頭再答覆你這件事。我必須要算一下。

好的。妳什麼時候可以給我們答覆呢？我們非常希望能儘早達成協議。

明天早上夠快了嗎？

那應該可以。

好的，那就這樣。我們內部會先談一下，然後明天第一時間打給你。

非常感謝，荷璞。

索取樣品
Request for Samples

I. 索取樣品一定要會的句型

✗ PLAY ALL | TRACK 118

句型1 〉 **表明來意**

The intent of this e-mail is to request samples of sth.

- The intent of this e-mail is to request samples of your porcelain floor tiles.

  這封信的目的是想向你索取地板磁磚的樣品。

....

句型2 〉 **樣品需求**

Please limit the samples to sth. (尺寸、規格)

- Please limit the samples to those sized 4x4 inches wide or smaller.

  請將這些樣品規格限制在四吋見方的大小，或是更小一點。

句型3 〉 **寄送地址**

Sth. may be delivered to the following address:

- The samples may be delivered to the following address:

  樣品可以寄到下面地址：

....

句型4 〉 **詢問費用**

Would you like to be reimbursed for sth.?

- Would you like to be reimbursed for the cost of the samples?

  你需要我們支付樣品的費用嗎？

II. 用 e-mail 索取樣品

To:	info@ttiles.com.tw
Subject:	Sample Request

Greetings,

表明來意 The intent of this e-mail is to request samples of **your porcelain floor tiles. We've heard good things about them, but would like to see for ourselves.** Please limit the

樣品需求 samples to **those sized 4x4 inches wide or smaller. We're not interested in large tiles. If we like what we see, we plan on placing a sizeable[1] order.**

寄送地點 The samples may be delivered to the following address:

523 Templeton Avenue
Greenwood, MI
07653 USA

詢問費用 Would you like to be reimbursed[2] for **the cost of the samples? We are more than willing to do so. If you prefer to have the samples returned to you, we can do that as well.**

Thank you for your time.

Sincerely,
Amanda Jackson, General Manager
Home Style Interiors

---------- 中文翻譯 ----------

收件人：info@ttiles.com.tw

主旨：索取樣品

你好：

這封信的目的是想向你索取地板磁磚的樣品。我們已經聽說許多關於此磁磚的優點，但還是想要親眼瞧一瞧。請將這些樣品規格限制在四吋見方的大小，或是更小一點。我們對大片磁磚不是很有興趣。如果我們對看到的商品滿意的話，我們打算要下一筆可觀的訂單。

樣品可以寄到下面地址：

07653 美國密西根州葛林伍德市
坦普雷頓大道五百二十三號

你需要我們支付樣品的費用嗎？我們非常樂意支付。如果你比較想要我們歸還樣品，我們也可以這麼做。

感謝你撥冗。

謹上

總經理　亞曼達·傑克森
室內居家風格設計

1. sizeable [ˈsaɪzəbəl] *adj.* 相當大的；可觀的

2. reimburse [ˌriəmˈbɜs] *v.* 償還；歸還

Ⅲ. 用 e-mail 回覆樣品索取

To: ajackson@homestyle.com

Subject: Re: Sample Request

Dear Ms. Jackson,

I will be happy to send you the samples you requested at no charge[1] whatsoever. In addition, we will include a full English catalog for your reference.[2] If you have any additional questions or would like to place an order, please don't hesitate to contact me. I will be happy to assist you in any way possible.

Sincerely,

Aaron Rao
Client Relations Representative
Taipei Tiles

收件人：ajackson@homestyle.com

主旨：回覆：索取樣品

親愛的傑克森小姐：

我很樂意寄給妳所要求的樣品且不收取任何費用。除此之外，我們附上全英文的型錄供妳參考。如果妳有其他疑問或是想下訂單的話，請不要客氣，儘管與我聯絡。我會很樂意在各方面協助妳。

謹上

饒亞倫
客戶關係代表
台北磁磚

1. charge [tʃɑrdʒ] *n.* 費用

2. reference [ˈrɛfərəns] *n.* 參考

Ⅳ. 電話索取樣品必備句

表明來意

A: **The reason I'm calling is to request some samples of your new dish racks.**

我打電話的原因是想索取一些你們新出的碗盤架的樣品。

B: **Which ones exactly? We've put a few new models out recently.**

精確來說是哪一種呢？我們最近推出了好幾款新的。

A: **How can I direct your call?**

請問要轉哪個部門呢？

B: **I'm calling to ask for some samples.**

我打來是想要索取一些樣品。

樣品需求

A: **Can you limit the samples to discount models only?**

你可以將樣品只限制在那些折扣商品嗎？

B: **Of course. We'll get those out to you sometime this afternoon.**

當然可以。今天下午我們就會將那些寄去給你。

A: **Which of our models were you interested in?**

你對我們哪些款式有興趣？

B: **We're interested in your line of protective headgear.**

我對你們的防護頭盔系列有興趣。

....

寄送地址

A: **Where should we send the samples? We don't have your address on file.**

我們應該將樣品寄到哪裡呢？我們檔案裡沒有你們的地址。

B: **Send them to this address. Are you ready?**

把它們寄到下列地址。你準備好了嗎？

....

詢問費用

A: **Are the samples complimentary or will you be billing us for them?**

這些樣品是免費的還是你會跟我們索取費用？

B: **We can send you <u>as many as</u> ten free samples.**

我們最多可寄十件免費樣品給你。

> 這裡的 as many as 也可以用 up to 來表示「最多」。

V. 用電話索取樣品

Matt: Good morning. Friendly Fabrics. This is Matt Tyler. How may I help you?

Debra: Good morning. My name is Debra Hsu from Asiatic Distributors. I'm calling to request samples of your fabrics. We'd be interested in making large orders if we like what we see.

Matt: We'd be happy to send you some samples. We have a wide range of fabrics available. What sort of material are you interested in?

Debra: A representative sampling would be best. And one more thing: Will there be a charge for the samples?

Matt: We don't charge for samples. They're rather small. Why don't you give me the address, and I'll have them shipped out this week?

Debra: Sounds good. Can I e-mail it to you?

Matt: Sure, that would probably be easier. Do you have my e-mail address?

Debra: Let me just verify that I have the right one: matt-underscore-tyler-at-friendly-fabrics-dot-com. Is that right?

Matt: That's me. I'll send you a reply as soon as I get the e-mail.

Debra: That's great, Thanks for your help.

Matt: Don't mention it. Have a good day.

經銷商代表黛伯拉打電話給布料供應商麥特，希望能索取一些樣品做參考。

早安。友善布料。我是麥特・泰勒。我可以怎麼幫妳？

早安。我是亞洲經銷商的徐黛伯拉。我打來是想索取布料樣品。如果我們看到樣品喜歡的話，就會有興趣下大筆訂單。

表明來意

我們很樂意寄給妳一些樣品。我們有多種布料可供選擇。妳對哪一種材質有興趣？

具代表性的樣品最好。還有件事：這些樣品有收取費用嗎？

樣品需求

詢問費用

我們樣品是不收費的。它們都很小。妳何不給我地址，然後我在這星期出貨？

聽起來不錯。可以用電子郵件寄給你嗎？

確實那樣或許會更方便。妳有我的電子郵件地址嗎？

讓我確認一下這地址是否正確：matt 底線 tyler-@-friendly-fabrics-dot-com。對嗎？

是我的沒錯。我收到郵件後會盡快向妳回覆。

太好了感謝你的幫忙。

不用客氣。祝妳有個愉快的一天。

通知價格調漲
Price Increase Announcement

I. 通知調漲一定要會的句型

✖ PLAY ALL | TRACK 123

句型1 > 漲價通知

We regret to inform you that . . .

- We regret to inform you that due to rising costs, we are no longer able to provide our fresh spring water at the same low prices.

  我們很遺憾要通知你，因為成本上漲的關係，我們無法再以同樣的低價來提供新鮮泉水。

句型2 > 調漲原因

Sth. + necessitate a rate adjustment effective + 日期

- The growing price of gasoline, combined with increased labor fees, necessitates a rate adjustment effective March 15.

  日漸上漲的油價，加上勞務費用的增加使我們必須從三月十五日起做價格調整。

句型3〉 **強調優勢**

As you know, sth. is your best source of . . .

■ As you know, Crystal Springs is your best source of crystal-clean drinking water.

如你所知，水晶泉水是純淨飲用水的最佳來源。

句型4〉 **招攬訂單**

Why not take this opportunity + to V.?

■ Why not take this opportunity to put an order in now while prices are still low?

何不趁價格還低的時候把握機會下訂單呢？

II. 用 e-mail 通知價格調漲

PLAY ALL | TRACK 124

To:	Vending Unlimited
Subject:	Rate Adjustment

Dear Valued Customer,

漲價通知

We regret to inform you that due to rising costs, we are no longer able to provide our fresh spring water at the same low prices. In today's economy, it has become impossible to produce and ship such high-quality water without increased costs. The growing price of gasoline, combined with increased labor fees, necessitates[1] a rate adjustment effective March 15. Despite these outside forces, we remain dedicated to making our water as affordable as possible. A summary of rate changes can be found in the accompanying[2] attachment.

調漲原因

We are sure you understand our commitment[3] to quality. As you know, Crystal Springs is your best source of crystal-clean drinking water. We go to great lengths to supply our customers with the best nature has to offer—straight from the Diamond Range Mountains to your glass.

強調優勢

We will be accepting orders at the normal rate until February 28. Why not take this opportunity to put an order in now while

招攬訂單

prices are still low? You won't regret it.

Drink well,

May Douglas, Customer Service Officer
Crystal Springs

中文翻譯

收件人：自動販賣無限公司

主旨：費用調整

致我們重視的客戶：

我們很遺憾要通知你，因為成本上漲的關係，我們無法再以同樣的低價提供新鮮泉水。以當今的經濟狀況，這種高品質的泉水要在不增加成本的情況下生產和運送是越來越不可能了。日漸上漲的油價，加上勞務費用的增加使我們必須從三月十五日起做價格調整。儘管有這些外部壓力，我們仍然致力使我們的水是大眾負擔得起的。價格變動的摘要可在隨附的檔案中找到。

我們確信你能瞭解我們對於品質的承諾。如你所知，水晶泉水是純淨飲用水的最佳來源。我們長途跋涉為客戶提供大自然的最佳獻禮——直接從鑽石山脈注入你的杯中。

在二月二十八號之前我們還是會接受平常價格的訂單。何不趁現在價格還低的時候把握機會下訂單呢？你不會後悔的。

多喝好水

客服人員　梅·道格拉斯
水晶泉水

1. necessitate [nɪˋsɛsəˌtet] v. 使成為必要

2. accompany [əˋkʌmpnɪ] v. 伴隨

3. commitment [kəˋmɪtmənt] n. 承諾；保證

III. 用 e-mail 回覆調漲通知

To: May Douglas

Subject: Re: Rate Adjustment

Dear Ms. Douglas,

We appreciate the timely[1] information. Given the coming rate adjustment, we would like to take advantage of your current prices by placing an order now for 100,000 500ml bottles of your Sparkling[2] Mineral Water. Please send us an invoice[3] and we will transfer the funds to your account. Thank you.

Regards,

Yolinda Chao, Inventory Manager
Vending Unlimited

收件人：梅‧道格拉斯

主旨：回覆：費用調整

親愛的道格拉斯小姐：

我們很感謝這個及時的資訊。假定價格即將調整，我們想利用你們現在的價格訂購十萬瓶五百毫升的氣泡礦泉水。請寄給我們一張發貨單，我們會將款項匯到妳的帳戶。謝謝。

謹上

存貨經理　曹尤琳達
自動販賣無限公司

1. **timely** [ˋtaɪmlɪ] *adj.* 及時的；適時的

2. **sparkling** [ˋspɑrkəlɪŋ] *adj.* 氣泡的

3. **invoice** [ˋɪnˌvɔɪs] *n.* 發貨單；發票

IV. 電話通知調漲必備句

漲價通知

A: **I'm sorry to inform you of a slight increase in our prices.**

我很遺憾要通知你價格有些微調整。

B: **You don't say! How much of an increase?**

不會吧！漲多少？

....

調漲原因

A: **Why are the prices going up?**

為什麼漲價了？

B: **It comes from rising gasoline prices. Everything is more expensive to ship.**

這是由於油價上漲。所有東西的運費都變更貴了。

> 價格調漲通常是因為成本增加，常見
> 的成本包括：生產成本（production
> cost）、勞務成本（labor cost）、運輸
> 成本（transportation cost）、燃料成本
> （fuel cost）。

強調優勢

A: You know as well as I do that **our whiteboard markers are the best on the market.**

你和我都知道我們的白板筆是市面上最棒的。

B: **They definitely are. We sell more of your brand than any other.**

確實是。和其他牌子比起來,你們的牌子我們是賣比較多。

A: As you are well aware, we are the leading name in **designer home furnishings.**

如同你所熟知的,我們是設計師家居裝潢的領導品牌。

B: **Yes, I agree. Your brand is indeed popular with our customers.**

是的,我同意。你們的牌子很受我們的客人喜愛。

招攬訂單

A: You might want to put an order in now **before the rate adjustment goes into effect.**

在價格調整生效之前,你可能會想要現在下訂單。

B: **That would probably be a good idea.**

那可能會是個好主意。

V. 用電話通知價格調漲

Neil: Hello, Sunny. It's Neil from Best Builders.

Sunny: Hi, Neil. Nice to hear from you. How've you been?

Neil: Not bad. Listen. I'm calling to follow up on an e-mail I sent you last week.

Sunny: I didn't get it. I've just got back from vacation and I haven't had time to go through all my e-mails yet. What was it about?

Neil: Unfortunately, we've had to slightly raise our prices across the board.

Sunny: Why the need for the rate adjustment?

Neil: Basically, it's the result of rising manufacturing costs. We've had to update our machinery and hire more workers.

Sunny: When does the increase take effect?

Neil: That's why I'm calling. The end of the month will be your last chance to get our products at their current prices. I thought you might not want to miss the opportunity.

Sunny: You're right. Let me write up an order and get back to you. Thanks for calling.

Neil: Thank you. You must have a lot to do. I'll let you go. Take care.

Sunny: Thanks again. Bye now.

頂尖建設的尼爾打電話通知老客戶價格即將全面調漲，希望他們能把握機會下單。

妳好，桑妮。我是頂尖建設的尼爾。

嗨，尼爾。很高興聽到你的消息。你最近如何？

還不錯。聽著。我打來是要追蹤我上星期寄給妳的信。

我沒有收到。我剛度假回來，還沒有時間去看我所有的電子郵件。是關於什麼事？

很遺憾，我們必須全面微調價格。 <kbd>漲價通知</kbd>

為什麼需要調整價格呢？

基本上，這是製造成本上漲的結果。我們必須更新我們的機器，並且僱用更多的工人。 <kbd>調漲原因</kbd>

調漲什麼時候生效？

這就是我打來的原因。本月底將是你們以目前價格訂購我們商品的最後機會。我想妳不會想錯失這次機會。 <kbd>招攬訂單</kbd>

你說的對。我來寫一份訂單然後回寄給你。謝謝你打來。

謝謝。妳一定還有很多事要做。我不打擾了。保重。

再次感謝。再見。

詢問其他付款方式
Request for Easier Payment Terms

I. 詢問其他付款方式一定要會的句型

✖ PLAY ALL | TRACK 128

句型1 說明情況

Please allow me to explain sth.

- Please allow me to explain our situation.
  請容我解釋一下我們的情況。

....

句型2 希望的付款方式

We prefer sth.（付款方式）

- For our international affairs, however, we prefer letters of credit.
  然而，對我們國際事務來說，我們比較希望使用信用狀。

句型3 **抱歉造成不便**

We apologize if . . .

- We apologize if this comes as an inconvenience to you.
  如果這會對你造成任何不便，我們在此表示歉意。

句型4 **等候回覆**

We await . . .

- We await your reply.
  我們等候你的回覆。

II. 用 e-mail 詢問其他付款方式

To: Tammy Zhao

Subject: Letter of Credit

Ms. Zhao,

說明情況

I'm writing to ask you for a favor. Please allow me to explain our situation. Normally, we make and receive payments to and from our bank account. For our domestic[1] business, this has proved convenient. For our international affairs,[2] however, we prefer

希望的付款方式

letters of credit. We apologize if this comes as an inconvenience to you. Please let us know if we can proceed with the order. If you have any questions or concerns, feel free to contact us.

抱歉造成不便

等候回覆

We await your reply.

letter of credit（信用狀）簡稱 LC 或 L/C，是國際貿易中最安全的付款方式之一。由於國際貿易中，往往不易掌握交易對象信用是否良好，而代表買方的外國銀行的信用是比較能讓人信賴的。其他如信用狀的開立銀行稱為 issuing bank、通知銀行則稱為 advising bank。

Sincerely,

John Edwards
Tiger Toys

收件人：趙泰咪

主旨：信用狀

趙小姐：

我寫信是想要請妳幫忙。請容我解釋一下我們的情況。一般情況下，我們是從銀行帳戶來支出和收取款項。對我們國內生意往來而言，這已證明相當便利。然而，對我們國際事務來說，我們比較希望使用信用狀。如果這會對妳造成任何不便我們在此表示歉意。如果訂單可以繼續進行的話，請讓我們知道。如果妳有任何問題或疑慮，隨時都可以聯絡我們。我們等候妳的回覆。

謹上

約翰・艾德華茲
老虎玩具

1. **domestic** [dəˋmɛstɪk] *adj.* 國內的

2. **affair** [əˋfɛr] *n.* 事務（通常為複數）

Ⅲ. 用 e-mail 回覆其他付款方式

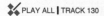

To: John Edwards

Subject: Re: Letter of Credit

Dear Mr. Edwards,

We would like to accommodate[1] your request to use a letter of credit. However, our accounting department is unfamiliar with this type of payment. We are afraid the process may be difficult to coordinate.[2] Since you have experience in this form of payment, perhaps you could explain it to us. We apologize for our inexperience[3] in this matter.

Sincerely,

Tammy Zhao
Taiwan Toys

收件人：約翰·艾德華茲

主旨：回覆：信用狀

親愛的艾德華茲先生：

我們願意順應你的需求使用信用狀。然而，我們的會計部門對於此種付款方式並不熟悉。我們擔心過程可能會難以協調。由於你們對此種付款方式有經驗，或許你們可以向我們說明。我們對這些事務缺乏經驗，在此表示歉意。

謹上

趙泰咪
台灣玩具

1. accomodate [əˋkɑməˏdet] v. 配合；順應

2. coordinate [koˋɔrdəˏnet] v. 協調一致

3. inexperience [ˏɪnɪkˋspɪriəns] n. 不熟練；無經驗

Ⅳ. 電話詢問付款方式必備句

說明情況

A: **What seems to be the problem?**

可能是怎麼樣的問題呢？

B: **Frankly, I'm not sure how to describe our situation.**

坦白說，我不太曉得該怎麼描述我們的狀況。

A: **Allow me to explain the circumstances we're facing.**

容我解釋一下我們正面臨的情況。

B: **Go ahead. I'm listening.**

請說。我在聽。

希望的付款方式

A: **How would you like to pay for the order?**

這筆訂單你想要怎麼付款？

B: **When it comes to larger orders our accountants prefer bank transfers.**

若是較大筆的訂單，我們會計人員比較喜歡的是銀行匯款。

> 付款方式包括 letter of credit（信用狀）、telegraphic transfer（電匯）、pay on delivery（貨到付款）、cash against documents（憑單付現）等。

A: **Would it be possible to pay in installments?**　有沒有可能分期付款呢？

B: We accept only **full payment up front** for international **orders.**　國際訂單我們只接受預付全額。

A: We are concerned about transfer fees.　我們擔心轉帳費用。

B: **You don't have to worry about that. There are none.**　那一點你不必擔心。不需要任何費用。

....

等後回覆

A: We are still waiting **to hear back from you.**　我們仍在等候你的回覆。

B: **Sorry about that. We've been flooded with orders lately.**　很抱歉。我們最近湧近很多的訂單。

V. 用電話詢問其他付款方式

Selina: Selina Song speaking. How may I help you?

Fred: Hi, Selina. My name is Fred Lenson from Lenson Piano Supply. I believe you have an order with us. Am I right?

Selina: That's right.

Fred: OK. I'm afraid we have a situation.

Selina: What seems to be the problem?

Fred: For international orders, I'm afraid I can't accept payment in installments. You'll have to make the entire payment up front.

Selina: I understand. Are you sure there is no way we can come to an agreement on this?

Fred: Unfortunately, not. I just can't accept the risk.

Selina: That's too bad. I may have to cancel my order entirely. At the very least, I will need to postpone it.

Fred: I don't mind putting the order on hold. Let me know when you are prepared to pay, and I'll process your order right away.

Selina: Thank you, Mr. Lenson.

Fred: You're welcome. Have a good day.

連森鋼琴供應商打電話告知客戶他們的國際訂單無法接受分期付款。

我是宋瑟琳娜。有什麼可以效勞的？

嗨，瑟琳娜。我是連森鋼琴供應商的佛萊德‧連森。我知道妳和我們有一筆訂單。對吧？

沒錯。

好的，恐怕我們有點狀況。　　　　　　　　　説明情況

是怎麼樣的問題呢？

對國際訂單來説，我恐怕無法接受分期付款。妳　　希望的付
必須事先付清全額。　　　　　　　　　　　　　款方式

我瞭解。你確定這件事我們沒有其他方法可以達成協議嗎？

很遺憾，沒有。我不能冒這個險。

那太糟了。我可能得將訂單全部取消了。至少，我得將訂單擱延。

我不介意暫緩這筆訂單。妳準備好方便付款的時　　等候回覆
候請讓我知道，我會立即處理妳的訂單。

謝謝你，連森先生。

不客氣。祝妳有個愉快的一天。

I. 下訂單一定要會的句型

✖ PLAY ALL | TRACK 133

句型1 〉 **訂購的商品**

I'd like to place an order for sth.（型號、規格等）

- I'd like to place an order for a number of your V-5A speakers.

  我想要訂購一些你們 V-5A 型的喇叭。

....

句型2 〉 **訂購數量**

We'd like to start with + 數量

- We'd like to start with an initial order of a thousand units.

  首筆訂單我們想訂購一千組。

句型3 > **詢價議價**

Would it be possible for you to lower the price if we ordered + 數量？

- Would it be possible for you to lower the price if we ordered a thousand speakers?
  如果我們訂一千個喇叭，你們有沒有可能把價格降低一點？

....

句型4 > **送件日期**

When is the earliest we can expect to receive sth.?

- When is the earliest we can expect to receive this order?
  我們最快何時可拿到這批貨呢？

II. 用 e-mail 下訂單

To:	Adam Horowitz
Subject:	Ordering Huppy Pup Chew Toys

Dear Mr. Horowitz,

訂購的商品

Following our phone conversation yesterday, I would like to place an order for your Happy Pup Chew Toys. I understand that the price for this product is $5.00 per unit.

訂購數量

However, since I intend to start with an order of 1,000 units,

詢價議價

would it be possible to lower the price? Please also let me know

送件日期

when would be the earliest I could expect to receive the products.

Thank you for your attention.

Regards,

Michael Diamond
Ace Pet Care Supplies

收件人：亞當・荷洛維茲

主旨：訂購快樂狗咀嚼玩具

親愛的荷洛維茲先生：

接續我們昨天在電話裡談論的話題，我想要訂購你們的快樂狗咀嚼玩具。我了解這商品每組價格為五塊美金。但是，因為我首批想要訂購一千組，有可能降低價格嗎？並請讓我知道最早什麼時候可以收到商品。

多謝關照。

謹上

邁可・戴蒙
首席寵物護理用品

文化補給站

看懂訂購單

訂購單（purchase order）上通常會有下列這些資訊，說明訂購商品、數量、價錢，以及交貨時間、方式等條件。以下是一些常見的用語：

Description: P/N (part number)	描述：產品編號
Quantity	數量
Unit Price	單價
amount	總計
Shipping Documents	出貨文件
Destination	目的地
Delivery	交貨期
Packing	裝運
remarks	附註

III. 用 e-mail 回覆下單

To: Michael Diamond

Subject: Re: Ordering Happy Pup Chew Toys

Dear Mr. Diamond,

Thank you for expressing your interest in Pet Plus's products. We would be happy to offer you a 10% discount from the listed price for an order of 1,000 units of our Happy Pup Chew Toys. Unfortunately, this item is currently out of stock.[1] We should, however, have it back in stock within three weeks. Our estimated[2] shipping time is 2–4 weeks.

打九折的英文	
✗	不是 ~~90% discount~~
✓	而是 10% discount

表示扣掉百分之十的價錢。你也可以說成 10% off。

If you would like to pre-order this product, please do not hesitate to contact me and I would be happy to assist you. My telephone number is: 123-445-5678.

Regards,

Adam Horowitz
Pet Plus

收件人：邁可・戴蒙

主旨：回覆：訂購快樂狗咀嚼玩具

親愛的戴蒙先生：

感謝您對寵愛寵物的產品表示興趣。關於一千件快樂狗咀嚼玩具的訂購，我們很樂意提供您標價九折的優惠。可惜，這件商品目前缺貨中。我們將會在三個星期內補貨。我們預估的出貨時間是二至四個星期。

如果您想要預訂此商品，請不要客氣儘管與我聯繫，我將很樂意為您服務。我的電話是 123-445-5678。

謹上

亞當・荷洛維茲
寵愛寵物

1. out of stock [aʊt] [əv] [stɑk] 無現貨的

2. estimate [ˈɛstəˌmet] *v.* 估計

IV. 電話下單必備句

訂購的商品

A: **Which model did you want to order?**

你想要訂哪一型？

B: **I'd like to place an order for your V-5A speakers, please.**

我想要訂購你們的 V-5A型喇叭。

....

訂購數量

A: **How many <u>pieces</u> are you looking at?**

你們打算訂多少件？

> 英文單位的説法除了 pieces/pcs、unit 之外還包括：bottle（瓶）、case（箱；盒）、drum（桶）、lot（批）等。

B: **We were thinking about an initial order of a thousand units.**

首批訂單我們想訂購一千組。

詢價議價

A: What are you charging for the basic model?

你們基本款的要價是多少？

B: Our listed price is US$100 per unit for the basic model.

我們基本款每組的標價是一百美元。

A: Would it be possible to lower the price if we ordered 1,000 speakers?

如果我們訂一千個喇叭，你們有沒有可能降價？

B: Unfortunately, our discounted prices start at a minimum order of 2,000 units. If you ordered 2,000 speakers, the price would be $80 per speaker.

很遺憾，我們的折扣價至少要訂購兩千組。如果你們訂購兩千個喇叭，那麼每個喇叭單價是八十美元。

送件日期

A: When is the earliest we can expect to receive this order?

我們最快何時可拿到這批貨呢？

B: I can get these out the door to you today—so, within a week.

我今天可以出貨給你——所以是一個星期以內。

V. 用電話下訂單

Nora: Clive? I'm glad I managed to catch you at your desk.

Clive: Hello, Nora. I was just going to call you about our new line of LED light bulbs.

Nora: Believe it or not, that's exactly why I'm calling. I'd like to place an order for those bulbs.

Clive: Great to hear it. What quantity are we looking at here?

Nora: We'd like to start with an order of a thousand cases. If they sell well, we'll increase this number down the line.

Clive: Understood. And we may be able to swing a discount for you if that happens.

Nora: When do you think we can receive this order?

Clive: I can get these out the door to you today— so within a week.

Nora: Perfect. We've got high hopes for these LED lights of yours, Clive.

Clive: They won't let you down, Nora.

DIY居家維修店買方代表諾拉致電給客戶克萊夫，準備下訂單。

克萊夫嗎？真高興我總算找到你了。

嗨，諾拉。我才正要打電話跟妳說我們新的LED燈泡系列。

不蓋你，這正是我打電話來的原因。我想訂購那些燈泡。

訂購的商品

很高興聽妳這麼說。這次考慮的數量是多少呢？

首筆訂單我們想訂購一千箱。如果銷路不錯，未來我們會增加數量。

訂購數量

瞭解了。如果訂單增加的話，我們有可能幫妳爭取到折扣。

你認為我們何時可拿到這批貨呢？

送件日期

我今天可以出貨給妳——所以是一個星期以內。

太棒了。我們對你們公司的LED燈泡寄予厚望喔，克萊夫。

諾拉，它們不會讓妳失望的。

I. 安排出貨一定要會的句型

✖ PLAY ALL | TRACK 138

句型1 提出問題

We still have a few questions about sth.

- We still have a few questions about some of the details.

  我們對某些細節還有一些問題。

句型2 運送日期

. . . provide us with an estimated delivery date.

- We hope you can provide us with an estimated delivery date.

  我們希望你可以提供我們一個預計的交貨日期。

句型3 出貨確認

Will we be getting a shipping confirmation . . . ?

- Will we be getting a shipping confirmation once our order leaves port?

  我們的貨物一離港時，我們會拿到出貨確認單嗎？

句型4 包裝需求

Would it be possible to + 包裝需求？

- Would it be possible to carefully wrap each unit in bubble wrap?

  可以每組都用氣泡紙仔細包裝嗎？

II. 用 e-mail 安排出貨

To: | Valerie Monroe
Subject: | Shipping Arrangements

Dear Ms. Monroe,

提出問題

We know that your company will be covering the cost of shipping for which we are grateful. We still have a few questions about some of the details, however. We are curious as to which shipping company you use. We would also like to know whether we will get a tracking[1] number associated with our order. In addition, we hope you can provide us with an estimated delivery

運送日期

date. We may need to expedite[2] our order.

出貨確認

Finally, will we be getting a shipping confirmation once our order leaves port?

包裝需求

We also have a special packaging request to ask of you. Would it be possible to carefully wrap each unit in bubble wrap? We've had orders from other companies get damaged in transit[3] and would like to avoid this happening again.

Thank you very much for <u>fielding</u> so many specific questions. We greatly appreciate your attention to our order.

> field 在此指的是回答
> 難以應付的問題，也可
> 用 cope with、address
> 來表示「應付」的意思。

Sincerely,

Yvonne Chen
Asia Pacific Producers, Inc.

──────── 中文翻譯 ────────

收件人：瓦樂莉・門羅

主旨：貨運安排

親愛的門羅小姐：

我們得知貴公司會負擔運費，對此我們深表感謝。然而，我們對某些細節還有一些問題。我們好奇你們使用的是哪一間貨運公司。我們也想知道我們是否會取得訂單的追蹤號碼。除此之外，我希望妳可以提供我們一個預計的交貨日期。這筆訂單我們可能會需要加快進行。最後，我們的貨物一離港時，我們會拿到出貨確認單嗎？

我們也有一些特殊的包裝要求要問妳。可以每組都用氣泡紙仔細包裝嗎？我們從其他公司訂購的貨物曾經在運送過程中受到損壞，希望能避免再發生此事。

非常感激妳回答這麼多細節問題。我們很感謝妳對我們貨物的關注。

謹上

陳依芳
太平洋亞洲製造有限公司

1. **track** [træk] *v.* 追蹤

2. **expedite** [ˈɛkspə͵daɪt] *v.* 迅速執行

3. **transit** [ˈtrænsət] *n.* 運送

Ⅲ. 用 e-mail 回覆出貨安排

✖ PLAY ALL | TRACK 140

To:	Yvonne Chen
Subject:	Re: Shipping Arrangements

Dear Ms. Chen,

We are more than happy to answer your questions.

Intercontinental Freight handles our shipping. They are an internationally ranked shipping company with a five-star rating. You can be assured that they will take good care of your order. A tracking number is indeed supplied for all our shipments. You will find it on the Shipping Confirmation which will be e-mailed to you promptly after your order leaves our warehouse. Once we ship your order, it should take approximately two weeks to reach you. We could ship as early as tomorrow, providing you have no further concerns. That will make the earliest arrival time August 9. I trust that meets with your approval?

As for your special request, you should know that we wrap all sensitive machine parts in bubble wrap and fill each container with Styrofoam pellets. We also use a very durable cardboard for our shipping containers. We have never had any problems with units damaged in shipping. Don't worry. Your order is in good hands.

It is our pleasure to serve you. If everything is to your liking, we can ship your order tomorrow. We await your reply.

Sincerely,

Valerie Monroe
Lincoln Machinery

中文翻譯

收件人：陳依芳

主旨：回覆：裝運安排

親愛的陳小姐：

我們很樂意回答妳的問題。

洲際貨運負責我們的運送。他們是列入國際排名的公司，有五顆星的等級。妳可以放心，他們一定會妥善處理妳的訂貨。事實上我們所有的貨物都有追蹤號碼。妳可以在運送確認單上找到，確認單會在訂貨離開我們倉庫後以電子郵件的方式立即傳送給妳。一旦我們將訂單裝貨運送，應該約莫兩個星期就會送達妳手上。倘若妳沒有其他疑慮的話，我們最早可以在明天出貨。這樣的話最早可以在八月九日抵達。我相信妳會贊同的，是嗎？

至於妳的特殊需求，妳應該知道我們會以氣泡紙仔細包裝所有靈敏的機械零件，並且將每個裝箱都填入保麗龍球。我們的運送箱也採用非常耐用的硬紙板。我們從未在運送過程中出現組件受損的問題。別擔心。妳的訂貨會受到妥善處理。

能替妳服務是我們的榮幸。如果每件事都合妳意的話，我們明天就可以出貨。等候妳的答覆。

謹上

瓦樂莉‧門羅
林肯機械

IV. 電話安排出貨必備句

提出問題

A: **Could we clarify some details in the shipping arrangements?**

我們可以釐清貨運安排上的一些細節嗎？

B: **Certainly. Which part of the shipping were you concerned about?**

當然。你們擔心運送的哪個部份？

....

運送日期

A: **When can we expect our shipment to arrive?**

我們能預期貨物什麼時候抵達嗎？

B: **It should be there no later than May 10.**

應該不會晚於五月十日。

出貨確認

A: Will we be getting an **e-mail** to confirm that **our shipment** has been sent out?

我們會收到電子郵件確認貨物已經寄出了嗎？

B: **We can provide that if you require it.**

如果你們要求的話我們可以提供。

A: Will you be sending us a shipment confirmation?

你會寄出貨確認通知給我們嗎？

B: **We will e-mail you a proof of shipment once the items have left our premises.**

一旦商品離開廠房我們就會以電子郵件寄出貨證明給你。

包裝需求

A: Would it be too much if we asked for nonstandard packaging?

如果我們要求非標準包裝會不會太過分？

B: **That depends on the nature of the packaging you require.**

那要看你們要求的是怎樣的包裝。

V. 用電話安排出貨

Ray: Hello. Ray Vicar speaking. How may I help you?

Nina: Hi, Ray. This is Nina from Emperor Music in Taiwan. I'm calling about our pending order. I wanted to discuss some of the shipping details with you.

Ray: Sure where should we start?

Nina: When can we expect the CDs to arrive?

Ray: They're going by air, so if we ship them on Monday, they should get there within three business days.

Nina: Excellent. So far, so good. Now I have a special request to ask of you.

Ray: I'm listening.

Nina: It's about the cases for the CDs. Could you possibly ship them in thick jewel cases and not the thin ones?

Ray: We can do it, but it will delay shipment by at least a week.

Nina: Not a problem. Thanks a lot.

Ray: My pleasure. Was there anything else?

Nina: No, that's it. Thanks again.

帝王音樂的妮娜打電話給雷‧維卡，詢問出貨的一些事宜。

妳好。我是雷‧維卡。我可以怎麼幫妳？

嗨，雷。我是從台灣帝王音樂打來的妮娜。我打　　提出問題
來是關於一筆尚未敲定的訂單。我想要跟你談談
一些運送細節。

當然。我們從哪裡開始？

我們可以預期這些CD什麼時候到？　　　　　　　運送日期

它們是走空運，所以如果我們星期一出貨的話，
應該會在三個工作天之內到達。

太棒了。目前為止都很好。現在我想向你提出一
個特殊要求。

請說。

是關於CD的盒子。可不可能用厚的CD硬殼出貨而　　包裝需求
不是用薄的那種嗎？

我們可以辦到，但是出貨至少要晚一個星期。

沒關係。非常謝謝。

這是我的榮幸。還有其他事嗎？

沒有，就這樣。再次感謝。

I. 催款一定要會的句型

✖ PLAY ALL ┃ TRACK 143

句型1 通知繳款到期

payment is now + 時間 + overdue.

- This letter is to inform you that payment is now three days overdue.

  這封信是要通知你們款項已經逾期三天了。

. . . .

句型2 提醒日期

Your payment of + 金額 + was due on + 日期

- Your payment of $5,356.89 was due on November 25.

  你們的款項，五千三百五十六點八九美元，在十一月二十五日到期。

句型3 **瞭解原因**

If you are unable + **to V.,** perhaps you could explain . . .

- If you are unable to make payment immediately or require special arrangements, perhaps you could explain the problem to us.

  如果你們無法立即付款或需要特殊安排，或許可以向我們說明問題。

句型4 **要求回覆**

We would appreciate hearing back from you . . .

- We would appreciate hearing back from you by phone or e-mail at your earliest convenience.

  若能儘早透過電話或電子郵件得到你們的回應，則不勝感激。

II. 用 e-mail 催款

| To: | Hearty Health (tom_trust@heartyhealth.com) |
| Subject: | Payment Reminder |

Dear Mr. Trust,

通知繳款到期

This letter is to inform you that your payment is now three days overdue. This regards your order of October 24 for 20 crates of multivitamins which was shipped to you on October 26 and delivered on November 18. Your payment of $5,356.89 was due on November 25. Please remit funds to our account for the balance mentioned above.

提醒日期

瞭解原因

We understand that it is sometimes difficult to make payment on time. If you are unable to make payment immediately or require special arrangements, perhaps you could explain the problem to us. Our accounting office has experience in solving difficult payment issues. We are happy to assist our customers whatever their needs may be.

要求回覆

We would appreciate hearing back from you by phone or e-mail at your earliest convenience. Thank you kindly.

Sincerely,

Jacky Fu
Vital Vitamins
886-2-2234-5678

─────── 中文翻譯 ───────

收件人：康健（tom_trust@heartyhealth.com）

主旨：付款通知

親愛的楚斯特先生：

這封信是要通知你的款項已經逾期三天了。這是有關你們在十月二十四日所訂購二十個貨櫃的綜合維他命，已於十月二十六日出貨並在十一月十八日到貨。你們的款項五千三百五十六點八九美元在十一月二十五日到期。請將上述的款項匯到我們的帳戶。

我們理解按時繳交款項有時候並不容易。如果你們無法立即付款或是需要特殊安排，或許可以向我們說明問題。我們的會計部門對於解決棘手的付款問題很有經驗。不管客戶的需求是什麼，我們都很樂意提供協助。

若能儘早透過電話或電子郵件得到你們的回應，則不勝感激。衷心感謝你。

謹上

傅傑克
活力維他命
886-2-2234-5678

Ⅲ. 用 e-mail 回覆催款

To: Jacky Fu (Vital Vitamins)

Subject: Re: Payment Reminder

Dear Mr. Fu,

Please accept my personal apologies for failing to make payment on time. I should have realized that the Thanksgiving holiday meant I needed to send payment earlier. Our offices were closed November 24 to the 27. Nevertheless, I should have anticipated[1] this problem and sent payment on Wednesday at the latest.[2] I hope we have not lost your trust. We will transfer the entire balance to your account immediately. We are sorry for the delay. Thank you for understanding.

Sincerely,

Tom Trust
Hearty Health

> transfer 表示「轉讓；轉移」的意思，可作名詞和動詞用，transfer the entire balance to your account 是指「將餘額轉帳到你的帳戶」的意思。另外 bank transfer 則指「銀行轉帳」，如 payment will be made by bank transfer（款項將以銀行轉帳方式來進行）。

收件人：傅傑克（活力維他命）

主旨：回覆：付款通知

親愛的傅先生：

對於沒有準時付款，請接受我個人道歉。我應該要知道感恩節假期表示我必須早點將款項寄出。我們十一月二十四日至二十七日期間不上班。儘管如此，我應該事先想到這個問題，並最晚在星期三寄出款項。我希望我們沒有失去你的信任。我們會立即將所有的剩餘款項匯到你們的戶頭。我很抱歉造成延遲。感謝你的諒解。

謹上

湯姆‧楚斯特
康健

1. anticipate [æn`tɪsə͵pet] *v.* 預想；預料

2. at the latest [æt] [ðə] [letɪst] *phr.* 最遲

IV. 電話催款必備句

通知繳款

A: Did you know that we haven't received payment for your latest invoice?

你知道我們沒有收到你們最近一筆發貨單上的款項嗎？

B: No, I wasn't aware of that. Let me look into that for you.

我不曉得這件事。讓我幫你查一查。

....

提醒日期

A: Your total of $43,789 was due a week ago today.

你們的總金額四萬三千七百八十九元的付款在一個星期前到期了。

B: That long?! We'll get that out to you as soon as possible.

有那麼久？我們會儘早給你。

A: When was the payment due?

款項是什麼時候到期？

B: It was due this past Monday which was April 30.

是在上個星期一，四月三十日到期。

瞭解原因

A: **Would you mind telling us the problem that led to the delay?**

你介意告訴我們是什麼問題導致延遲的嗎？

B: **It seems our accountant provided the wrong information to the bank.**

好像是我們的會計人員提供給銀行的資訊是錯的。

要求回覆

A: **We would appreciate an answer as soon as possible.**

如蒙儘早回覆將不勝感激。

B: **I'll find out and get back to you right away.**

我會查明並立即回覆你。

> 催款時必須要提到幾個重要的時間：開票日（billing date）、到期日（due date）、發貨單日期（invoice date）。

V. 用電話催款

Adam: Hello, Laura. This is Adam from Creative Décor.

Laura: Hi, Adam. Thanks for sending us those statuettes. What can I do for you?

Adam: Actually, that order is why I'm calling. We haven't received your payment yet.

Laura: I had no idea. How long is it overdue?

Adam: Almost a week now.

Laura: My apologies, Adam. I'll get right on it.

Adam: Do you have any idea how this could have happened?

Laura: Not yet. I'm as surprised as you are. I'll definitely be having a word with my secretary.

Adam: Thanks, Laura. I appreciate your taking care of it.

Laura: I'll make sure you have the payment ASAP. I'm sorry for the trouble.

Adam: It's OK. I'll let you go now, so you can work things out. Thanks again.

創意室內裝潢的亞當打電話給客戶通知繳款逾期，並試著瞭解逾期的原因。

妳好，蘿拉。我是創意室內裝潢的亞當。

嗨，亞當。感謝你寄給我們那些雕像裝飾。我可以為你做什麼嗎？

其實，我打來就是為了那筆訂單。我們還沒收到你們的付款。

通知繳款到期

我不清楚。逾期多久了？

到現在差不多一星期了。

亞當，我很抱歉。我會馬上處理。

妳知道為什麼會發生這種事嗎？

瞭解原因

還不曉得。我和你一樣驚訝。我一定會和我的祕書談一談。

謝謝妳，蘿拉。我很感謝妳要處理這件事。

我會確認你儘早收到款項。我很抱歉造成你的麻煩。

沒關係。我要掛了，這樣妳才可以處理這件事。再次感謝。

>>> *Notes*

310

售後處理篇

貿易往來難免要處理售後的問題,無論是處理退貨、賠償的問題,或要求技術支援,這些都是相當實用的議題。該如何向客戶說明原因以取得對方諒解,或是在維護公司權益下又不傷害彼此貿易關係?在這個篇章中我們要告訴你各種應對的技巧。

26 | 更改訂單
Changing an Order

I. 更改訂單一定要會的句型

✖ PLAY ALL | TRACK 148

句型1 > **是否能更改訂單**

We would like + to V. if at all possible.

- We would like to increase our order if at all possible.

  如果可能的話我們想要增加訂量。

句型2 > **更改原因**

This is due to sth.

- This is due to new market analyses which suggest a stronger demand than we at first anticipated.

  這是因為新的市場分析顯示，需求比我們原先預期的還要更大量。

句型3 **詢問價錢**

Please inform us of **sth.**

- Please inform us of the new price.
  請告知我們最新價錢。

II. 用 e-mail 更改訂單

To: | Allen Wilson

Subject: | URGENT: Order Change

Dear Mr. Wilson,

I realize we have already finalized[1] the order (invoice #02318), and you may have already shipped it. However, it has come to our attention that we will need more of the same item. We would like to increase our order if at all possible.

> sth. comes to sb.'s attention 通常表示注意到某個問題。

是否能更改訂單

更改原因

This is due to new market analyses which suggest a stronger demand than we at first anticipated. As such, could you double our order to 100,000 units? Everything else on the order remains the same.

You said something during our negotiations about a discount for larger orders. I can't remember now what the minimum[2] order was to obtain a lower rate. Does our order qualify now? Please inform us of the new price either way. We apologize for the inconvenience. Thank you.

詢問價錢

Sincerely,

Ethan Chen
Asia-Pacific Conglomerates,[3] Inc.

收件人：艾倫・威爾森

主旨：緊急：更改訂單

親愛的威爾森先生：

我知道我們已經完成這份訂單（發貨單 02318 號），而你可能已經出貨。然而，我們剛注意到我們需要更多相同的商品。如果可能的話我們想要增加訂量。這是因為新的市場分析，顯示需求比我們原先預期的還要更大。如上所述，你可以將我們的訂量增加一倍到十萬組嗎？訂單上的其他條件維持不變。

在我們議價的過程中你有提到大量訂購的折扣。我現在不記得符合較低價錢的最少訂量是多少。我們現在的訂單有符合條件了嗎？用哪種方式都可以，請告知我們最新的價錢。我們對於造成不便感到抱歉。謝謝你。

謹上

陳伊森
亞洲太平洋企業集團

1. finalize [ˈfaɪnəˌlaɪz] v. 結束；完成

2. minimum [ˈmɪnəməm] adj. 最少的

3. conglomerate [kənˈɡlɑmrət] n. 企業集團

III. 用 e-mail 回覆訂單修改

To:	Ethan Chen
Subject:	Re: URGENT: Order Change

Dear Mr. Chen,

I'm pleased to inform you that we caught the shipment in time, though just barely.[1] Our driver was just about to leave the warehouse with your order! Fortunately, we stopped him and filled his truck with the double order you asked for. To answer your question: Yes, your order now qualifies for the 10% discount we discussed earlier. We will apply[2] it to the new invoice (#02319) which you can find attached to this e-mail. Your total is now US$80,000.

Thank you for your business and your increased order.

Sincerely,

Allen Wilson
Great Things

收件人：陳伊森

主旨：回覆：緊急：更改訂單

親愛的陳先生：

我很高興通知你我們及時將貨品攔下，只差了一步。我們司機剛好要將你訂的貨運離倉庫！幸好，我們攔住他，並將你們要求的兩倍訂單上貨。回覆你的問題：是的，你的訂單現在符合我們先前提過的九折優惠。我們會在新的發貨單（#02319）上做折扣，你可以在此封信件的附檔中找到。現在總價是八萬美金。

感謝此次交易以及所追加的訂單。

謹上

艾倫·威爾森
絕妙好事

1. barely [ˋbɛrli] *adv.* 勉強地

2. apply [əˋplaɪ] *v.* 使適用

Ⅳ. 電話更改訂單必備句

是否能更改訂單

A: **We would like to add a few items to our order if that's OK.**

如果沒問題的話，我們想要在訂單中增加一些品項。

B: **Certainly. We can just draw up a new invoice for you.**

當然。我們可以再擬一份新的發貨單給你。

A: **We need to make some changes to the order.**

我們需要將訂單做一些修改。

B: **What sort of changes did you have in mind?**

你想要做什麼樣的修改？

....

更改原因

A: **Why the change of heart?**

為什麼改變心意？

B: **No change of heart. It's actually because of a clerical error on our part.**

沒有改變心意。其實是因為我們這邊筆誤。

A: **The change is due to an oversight in planning which we've just now caught.**

修改是因為在計畫時有所疏失，我們現在才注意到。

B: **That's not a problem. Let's write you up a new order.**

沒問題。我們再幫你寫一份新的訂單。

> 更改訂單（change an order）常見的原因有：消費者需求（consumer demand）、為符合需求（to meet demand）、筆誤（clerical error）、天災（natural disaster）、匯率變動（change in currency rate）、倉庫空間改變（change in warehouse space）、國內情勢改變（change in domestic situation）等等。

詢問價錢

A: **How will this change the price?**

這項更動會影響價錢嗎？

B: **The rate should stay the same.**

價錢應該會維持不變。

V. 用電話更改訂單

Fiona:	Hello, Mr. Twain? This is Fiona Sun from Taipei Imports in Taiwan. We have an active order with you.
Eddie:	Hello, Ms. Sun. Could you give me the number on the invoice?
Fiona:	Of course. I have it right here. It's 10498.
Eddie:	OK. Here it is. You ordered 1,000 sheets of leather, is that right?
Fiona:	Correct. But we'd like to change that order to 2,000 sheets if that's OK.
Eddie:	That should be alright. We haven't shipped your order out yet. Any reason for the sudden change?
Fiona:	It seems we can save money on shipping if we order more.
Eddie:	That's always good.
Fiona:	Indeed. I presume this shouldn't affect the price at all? Or would you like to give us a discount by any chance?
Eddie:	I'm sorry. We've actually already given you the discounted rate.
Fiona:	I understand. Never hurts to ask, though. Well then, thanks for the help, Mr. Twain. It's been a pleasure.
Eddie:	Thank you, Ms. Sun. We'll get this shipment out to you right away.

> 在商業電話禮儀中，為了感謝別人的協助，在結束電話前可以跟對方說 it's been a pleasure，或是 it's been a pleasure talking to you。

台北進口公司的菲歐娜打電話詢問廠商是否能增加訂單，以及是否有額外折扣。

你好？吐溫先生？我是從台灣的台北進口公司打來的孫菲歐娜。我們和你們有一份進行中的訂單。

妳好，孫小姐。妳可以給我發貨單號碼嗎？

當然。我這裡有。是一〇四九八。

好的。在這裡。你們訂購了一千張毛皮，對嗎？

正確。如果可以的話，我們想要將訂單改成兩千張。

是否能
更改訂單

那應該沒問題。你們訂單我們還沒出貨。突然更動是有什麼原因嗎？

如果我們訂多一點的話，似乎可以節省運費。

更改原因

那總是好的。

確實。我猜想這一點並不會影響價錢吧？或是你可能願意給我們一些折扣？

詢問價錢

我很抱歉。我們事實上已經給你們折扣價了。

我瞭解。問問而已不打緊。那麼吐溫先生，感謝你的協助。我很榮幸。

謝謝妳，孫小姐。我們會立即出貨給妳的。

運送延誤
Shipment Delay

I. 說明運送延誤一定要會的句型

✖ PLAY ALL | TRACK 153

句型1 〉 無法如期履約

I'm sorry to inform you that . . . by + 時間

- I'm sorry to inform you that we will not be able to complete your order by the date stipulated in the contract.

  我很遺憾通知你我們沒有辦法按照合約中所約定的日期來完成你的訂單。

....

句型2 〉 運送問題

Sth. has caused damage to sth.

- A serious typhoon has caused extensive damage to local infrastructure.

  颱風對本地公共建設造成大規模的破壞。

句型3 〉 **預估交貨日期**

We expect your order can be shipped as early as + 日期

- We expect your order can be shipped as early as August 14.

  我們預期你們的訂單最早可以在八月十四日出貨。

....

句型4 〉 **道歉並提供協助**

Please accept my apologies and feel free to contact me . . .

- Please accept my apologies and feel free to contact me if you have any questions or issues you would like me to address.

  請接受我的道歉，如果你有任何疑問或是有任何需要我處理的問題請隨時跟我聯絡。

II. 用 e-mail 說明運送延誤

To:	Lance Carrols
Subject:	Production/Shipment Delay

Dear Mr. Carrols,

無法如期履約

I'm sorry to inform you that we will not be able to complete your order by the date stipulated[1] in the contract. A serious typhoon recently came through our area of

運送問題

Taiwan. It has caused extensive damage to local infrastructure.[2] In particular, a large landslide has blocked the access road to our factory, making it impossible for workers to get there.

We have yet to assess[3] the damage at the factory itself, but we are hopeful that production can continue as soon as the road is cleared. We will update you on developments as soon as there are any.

預估交貨日期

As it stands, we expect your order can be shipped as early as August 14. Be advised, however, this is merely an estimate.

道歉並提供協助

Please accept my apologies and feel free to contact me if you have any questions or issues you would like me to address.

Sincerely,

Michael Meng
Taitung Transistors

────── **中文翻譯** ──────

收件人：蘭斯・卡洛斯

主旨：生產／運送延遲

親愛的卡洛斯先生：

我很遺憾通知你我們沒有辦法按照合約中所約定的日期來完成你的訂單。最近有個強烈颱風通過我們台灣這一區，而對本地公共建設造成大規模的破壞。尤其，一場大規模的山崩阻擋了我們往工廠的道路，讓我們的工人無法到達那裡。

我們還沒辦法評估工廠本身的損失，但希望道路一疏通後就能繼續生產。一旦有任何進展我們就會儘快告知你。以目前的狀況來看，我們希望你的訂單最早可以在八月十四日出貨。然而必須告知你，這只是我們的預估。

請接受我的道歉，如果你有任何疑問或是有任何需要我處理的問題請隨時跟我聯絡。

謹上

孟邁克
台東電晶體

1. stipulate [ˈstɪpjəˌlet] *v.* (合約) 規定

2. infrastructure [ˈɪnfrəˌstrʌktʃə] *n.* 公共設施

3. assess [əˈsɛs] *v.* 評估

Ⅲ. 用 e-mail 回覆運送延誤

To: | Michael Meng

Subject: | Re: Production/Shipment Delay

Dear Mr. Meng,

I am sorry to hear about the difficulties you are experiencing in your country. We at Caltronics wish you the best as you attempt to recover from this natural disaster. The delay in shipment should not cause a problem for us. We are merely filling our inventory. Based on current sales patterns though, we do expect to need the shipment by early October or so. If our order cannot be completed in its entirety by then, perhaps we could arrange a partial shipment. We understand that this must be a difficult situation for you, so we only ask that you keep us informed. Thank you.

Again, good luck in your clean-up effort.

Sincerely,

Lance Carrols
Caltronics

收件人：孟邁克

主旨：回覆：生產／運送延遲

親愛的孟先生：

很遺憾聽到你們國家所遭遇的艱難處境。當你們努力從天然災害中復原時，卡爾電子也祝福你們一切順利。交貨時間的耽擱對我們應該不會造成問題。我們只是要補充庫存。但依照目前的銷售模式來看，我們預期十月初左右會需要這批貨。如果到時候我們的訂單無法全部完成，或許我們可以安排部份出貨。我們理解這對你們而言一定是很困難的處境，所以我們只要求隨時告知我們最新的消息。謝謝你。

再次祝你們的清理工作順利。

謹上

蘭斯‧卡洛斯

卡爾電子

Ⅳ. 電話說明運送延誤必備句

PLAY ALL | TRACK 156

運送問題

A: It's come to my attention that there is a problem with the shipping address we have on file.

我注意到我們檔案上的寄送地址有問題。

B: I think we can help you fix that.

我想我們可以幫你們修正。

....

預估交貨日期

A: We expect to have your order ready for shipment no later than June 23.

我們希望可以將你們的訂單在六月二十三日前準備好出貨。

B: So can you guarantee delivery by July 10?

所以你們可以保證在七月十日前交貨嗎？

A: When can we expect delivery?

預估何時可以交貨？

B: That depends on how soon we can get the raw materials for production.

那得看我們能多快拿到生產用的原物料。

A: **We need to have those units no later than October 25.**

我們需要在十月二十五日之前收到這些組件。

B: **We'll <u>see to it that</u> you have them by then.**

我們務必會讓你們在那之前收到。

> see to 表示「負責;處理」的意思,see to it that S. + V. 則表示「確保……」。

道歉

A: **Please accept our sincere apologies for the inconvenience.**

對於造成不便,請接受我們誠摯的道歉。

B: **We understand. We're sure you'll do your best to get the shipment to us as quickly as possible.**

我們瞭解,相信你們會盡全力儘快出貨給我們。

V. 用電話說明運送延誤

Victor: Hello. Is this Ms. Tsai?

Ali: It is. Who may I ask is calling?

Victor: My name is Victor Danse. I'm in charge of overseeing international orders here at Tyson Tape. You ordered 5,000 rolls of industrial grade tape from us, is that right?

Ali: That is correct. What can I help you with today, Mr. Danse?

Victor: Well, we may have a problem getting your order to you on time. A key piece of equipment in our factory has broken down and needs to be replaced.

Ali: That's unfortunate. How long of a delay do you expect there to be?

Victor: We expect your order to be delayed by a week or two at most.

Ali: I see. We will have to reorganize some of our plans, but it should be feasible.

Victor: Please accept our apologies for the inconvenience.

Ali: It's OK. You have a great product, and we would be wise to wait for it.

Victor: Thank you for understanding. If you have any questions, just drop me a line or send me an e-mail.

Ali: Thanks for the heads-up. Take care.

泰森膠帶的維克特打電話通知客戶運送會耽擱，並解釋耽擱原因。

妳好，是蔡小姐嗎？

是的，請問你是哪位？

我是維克特‧丹斯。我負責監管泰森膠帶的國際訂單。你們向我們訂購了五千捲工業級膠帶，對嗎？

沒錯。丹斯先生，我今天可以幫你什麼忙呢？

是這樣的，我們可能無法準時交貨。我們工廠裡的一個主要設備壞掉了，需要更換。　　　無法如期
　　　　　　　　　　　　　　　　　　　　　　履約

那太遺憾了。你們預估會延遲多久？

我們預估會晚一個星期、或最多兩個星期才能交貨。　　　　　　　　　　　　　　　預估交貨
　　　　　　　　　　　　　　　　　　　　　　日期

我瞭解了。我們需要將一些計畫重新安排，但應該是可行的。

造成不便請見諒。　　　　　　　　　　　　道歉

沒關係。你們的產品很棒，我們為此等待是明智的。

感謝妳的體諒。如果妳有任何問題，儘管寄短信或寄電子郵件給我。

謝謝你的提醒。保重。

I. 退貨一定要會的句型

✖ PLAY ALL | TRACK 158

句型1 〉 **發現瑕庛品**

It has come to our attention that . . .

- It has come to our attention that your recent shipment of drinking glasses contains defective merchandise.

  我們注意到你們最近這批玻璃水杯有瑕疵品。

句型2 〉 **商品瑕疵狀況**

Sth. have been found to have sth. （瑕疵狀況）

- As many as three glasses per crate have been found to have bubbles, cooling marks or sand deposits.

  每一箱中就發現多達三個杯子有氣泡、冷卻痕或是沙子沉澱。

句型3 **要求退貨**

We cordially request a return of **sth.**

- We cordially request a return of this shipment.
  我們誠摯要求退回這批貨。

....

句型4 **下次交貨日期**

Could we expect delivery of the new shipment by + 日期?

- Could we expect delivery of the new shipment by December 15?
  我們可以預計在十二月十五日前收到新貨嗎？

II. 用 e-mail 要求退貨

To: Greta Kuo

Subject: Defective Merchandise

Dear Ms. Kuo,

發現瑕疵商品

It has come to our attention that your recent shipment of drinking glasses contains defective merchandise. We are extremely disappointed in the quality of work represented therein.[1] As many as three glasses per crate[2] have been found to have bubbles, cooling marks or sand deposits.[3]

商品瑕疵狀況

要求退貨

We consider this amount unacceptable. As such, we cordially[4] request a return of this shipment.

下次交貨日期

This order was confirmed on October 6 and received yesterday. We calculate approximately five to six weeks for delivery of a new, non-defective shipment. Could we expect delivery of the new shipment by December 15?

Thank you kindly for your attention to this matter.

Sincerely,

Joseph Holder
Discount Glassware

334

收件人：郭格蕾塔

主旨：瑕疵商品

親愛的郭小姐：

我們注意到你們最近這批玻璃水杯有瑕疵品，對於商品的品質在這點上我們感到極度失望。每一箱就發現多達三個杯子有氣泡、冷卻痕或是沙子沉澱，我們難以接受這樣的數量。因此我們誠摯要求退回這批貨。

這筆訂單是在十月六日確認並在昨天收到。我們估算一批新的、無瑕疵的貨品約需五至六個星期到貨。我們可以預計在十二月十五日前收到新貨嗎？

衷心感謝妳關切此問題。

謹上

喬瑟夫・侯德
美廉玻璃器皿

1. therein [ðɛrˋɪn] *adv.* 在那一點上

2. crate [kret] *n.* 板條箱；箱

3. deposit [dɪˋpɑzət] *n.* 沉澱物

4. cordially [ˋkɔrdʒəli] *adv.* 衷心地；誠懇地

Ⅲ. 用 e-mail 回覆退貨

PLAY ALL | TRACK 160

To: | Joseph Holder

Subject: | Re: Defective Merchandise

Dear Mr. Holder,

We are very sorry that you were disappointed in the quality of the glassware you received from us. Our workers do their best to prevent defects at all points of production.

Despite this fact, we are unable to accept your request for a return. First, it is impossible to prevent defects in all units. It would be foolish to discard[1] usable items merely because they are aesthetically[2] imperfect. Secondly, our quality assurance team inspects all of our shipped products carefully. It is unlikely that they have made many mistakes. Finally, please refer to Section 24B of our contract agreement which states: "Imperfections, including small bubbles, straw marks or cooling marks, are considered acceptable as long as they do not occur in more than 5% of the shipped product." Since there are exactly 100 units in each crate, three per crate is well below the contractual limit.

Absent a breach of contract on our part, we will not be accepting a return on this shipment.

If you would like to discuss this issue further, please call me at my office. Thank you very much.

Regards,

Greta Kuo
Taiwan Glass Co.
886-3-3498-6432

─────────── 中文翻譯 ───────────

收件人：喬瑟夫·侯德

主旨：回覆：瑕疵商品

親愛的侯德先生：

很遺憾你對我們寄去的玻璃杯品質感到失望。我們的工人在每個生產環節上都盡全力避免瑕疵。

儘管如此，我們仍無法接受你的退貨要求。首先，要避免所有的組件沒有瑕疵是不可能的。只因為在美觀上有瑕疵就拋棄這些可用的商品是不明智的。第二，我們的品管團隊都非常仔細檢查我們所有的出貨商品，他們應該不可能出這麼多的錯。最後，請參考我們合約協議上第二十四條 B 所列：瑕疵商品包括小氣泡、燒痕或冷卻痕的發生率在出貨商品中只要未達百分之五都被視為可接受。由於每箱剛好有一百組，每箱三個則遠低於合約上的限制。

我方並沒有違反合約，我們將無法接受退貨。如果你想要進一步討論這個問題，請打我辦公室的電話。感激不盡。

謹上

郭格蕾塔
台灣玻璃器公司
886-3-3498-6432

1. discard [dɪsˋkɑrd] v. 拋棄

2. aesthetically [ɛsˋθɛtɪklɪ] adv. 美學觀點地

Ⅳ. 電話退貨必備句

商品瑕疵狀況

A: **We are not happy with the quality of the merchandise you sent us.**

對於你們寄來的商品品質我們不是很滿意。

B: **I'm sorry to hear that. What didn't you like about it?**

我很遺憾聽到那樣的事。你們哪一點不滿意？

A: **More than a few of the product labels had spelling or grammatical errors.**

很多產品標籤上有拼字或文法錯誤。

B: **Really? I don't see how that is possible.**

真的嗎？我看是不太可能的。

A: **What sort of defects did you find in the products?**

你在商品中發現什麼樣的瑕疵？

B: **We found misplaced stickers and faded typeface.**

我們發現貼紙貼錯位置而且字體還褪色。

要求退貨

A: We ask that you grant us a return on this order.

我們請你們同意退回這筆訂單。

B: I'm afraid I'll need more information before I can say yes or no on that.

恐怕我還需要更多訊息才能告訴你可以不可以。

....

下次交貨日期

A: How soon do you expect you could send us our return?

你預期多快可以將退貨商品寄給我們？

B: Assuming we accept your request, in approximately three days.

假使我們接受你們的要求，大概要三天。

V. 用電話要求退貨

Adam:	Hello. Is Lydia Hsu there, please?
Lydia:	This is she. How may I help you?
Adam:	My name is Adam East from Parker Plumbing Supply. We ordered some copper joints from you.
Lydia:	Yes. How can I help you Mr. East?
Adam:	Well, there's a problem with the joints you sent us. They're defective.
Lydia:	That's impossible. What sort of defect are you referring to?
Adam:	They do not fit the pipes we intended to use them with.
Lydia:	Perhaps you gave us the wrong specifications.
Adam:	I don't think so. I reviewed the specifications myself. We would like a return of these joints for correct ones.
Lydia:	Before we can accept a return, we'll have to see definitive proof that we've made a mistake.
Adam:	In that case, it might be prudent to send a representative here to help us figure out the mistake. What do you think?
Lydia:	I'll have to get back to you on that. Could I let you know tomorrow?
Adam:	That would be fine. Thank you for your time.
Lydia:	Not at all. Have a good day, sir.

帕克配管供應商代表亞當打電話給廠商，表示收到的貨品規格不符，希望能退貨。

妳好，請問徐莉迪雅在嗎？

我就是，請問有什麼需要幫忙的嗎？

我是從帕克配管供應商打來的，我的名字是亞當‧伊斯特。我們向你們訂購了一些銅製接合器。

是的。有什麼需要幫忙的嗎，伊斯特先生？

是這樣的，你們送來的接合器有一些問題，它們有瑕疵。

> 發現瑕疵品

那是不可能的。你指的是哪一種瑕疵？

它們無法安裝在我們想要使用的管子上。

> 商品瑕疵狀況

或許你們給我們的規格是錯誤的。

我不這麼認為，我自己檢查過規格。我們想將這些接合器換成正確的。

> 要求退貨

在我們接受退貨之前，我們必須要看到確切證據證明出錯的是我們。

那麼為了謹慎起見，你們可以派一位代表來幫我們找出錯誤。妳覺得如何？

這事我必須回頭再跟你說。我可以明天告訴你嗎？

那應該可以。謝謝妳撥空處理。

一點也不會。先生，祝你有個愉快的一天。

I. 要求賠償一定要會的句型

✖ PLAY ALL | TRACK 163

句型1 > **要求賠償**

. . . and we are filing a claim + to V.

- The machine is malfunctioning, and we are filing a claim to replace it.

機器故障了，我們要求更換。

....

句型2 > **狀況說明**

The technician was unable to solve the problem and told us that + S. + V.

- The technician was unable to solve the problem and told us that the machine may have been improperly assembled.

這位技師無法解決問題並告訴我們機器可能組裝不當。

句型3 **造成損失**

As a result of this issue, we are losing sth. and have had to pay for . . .

- As a result of this issue, we are losing production time and have had to pay for a technician to come in.

因為這個問題，我們損失了生產時間，還需要付錢請技術人員來。

....

句型4 **賠償項目**

We would like you to + **V.** as well as . . .

- We would like you to replace the malfunctioning unit as well as reimburse us for the technician's fee and lost production time.

我們想要你們更換故障的組件且賠償我們技師費用及生產時間的損失。

II. 用 e-mail 要求賠償

To:	Harry Rao
Subject:	Malfunctioning Machine

Dear Mr. Rao,

要求賠償
This e-mail is to inform you of a problem we've encountered with the T2000 packaging machine we bought from your company. The machine is malfunctioning, and we are filing a claim to replace it. After having it installed by a certified[1] technician, the machine worked fine for a few weeks. Following a storm in which the factory lost power, our personnel found that the error light was on. We called in a professional to fix it.

狀況說明
The technician was unable to solve the problem and told us that the machine may <u>have been improperly assembled.</u>[2]

> 在抱怨貨物品質時,可用被動的語氣委婉暗示誰該負責,在雙方都心知肚明的情況下盡量避免指名道姓,這是談判技巧之一。

造成損失
As a result of this issue, we are losing production time and have had to pay for a technician to come in. We need to get a functioning machine installed as quickly as possible.

賠償項目
We would like you to replace the malfunctioning unit as well as reimburse us for the technician's fee and lost production

time.

We hope that you can reply promptly since every day spent is more product we are unable to package and ship. Thank you.

Sincerely,

Erin Satchel
Super Snacks

中文翻譯

收件人：羅哈利

主旨：機器故障

親愛的羅先生：

這封信是要告知你，我們最近向貴公司購買的 T2000 包裝機遇到了問題。機器故障了，我們要求更換。在合格技師組裝過後，機器正常運作了幾個星期。接著在一次暴風雨造成工廠斷電後，我們的同仁發現錯誤燈號亮起。我們打電話找了一位專家來修理。這位技師無法解決問題並告訴我們機器可能組裝不當。

因為這個問題，我們損失了生產時間，還需要付錢請技術人員來。我們需要盡快有一台組裝好能運作的機器。我們想要你們更換故障的組件，並且賠償我們技師費用以及生產時間的損失。

我們希望你們能立即回覆，因為每多花一天的時間，我們就有更多的產品無法包裝運送。謝謝你。

謹上

艾琳‧莎翠爾
超級點心

1. certified [ˋsɝtəˌfaɪd] *adj.* 認證的

2. assemble [əˋsɛmbəl] *v.* 組裝

Ⅲ. 用 e-mail 回覆賠償要求

To: Erin Satchel

Subject: Re: Malfunctioning Machine

Ms. Satchel,

We are sorry to hear that you have been experiencing difficulty with our T2000 packaging machine. It's always ideal to avoid additional expenses whenever possible. Unfortunately, we cannot accept your claim for a return.

It is clear from your description what the problem is. Having lost power and not being shut down properly, the machine required a reboot. If not done precisely, the T2000 may not function. The technician you hired was likely unaware of this. We suggest you refer to the manual supplied with the machine. Pages 115–119 detail the proper procedure for rebooting your T2000. I've attached a copy of the English version of the manual for your convenience. Please have a look.

We understand your frustration. Hopefully, our advice will prove useful. It is our duty and our pleasure to guide you through any technical problems you may have with our machines. We trust that you can resolve the problem with our guidance. If you have any questions or concerns, please do not hesitate to contact me again.

Best Regards,

Harry Rao
Taoyuan Packing Corp.

中文翻譯

收件人：艾琳‧莎翠爾

主旨：回覆：機器故障

莎翠爾小姐：

我們很遺憾聽到你們在使用我們 T2000 包裝機時遭遇困難。不管什麼時候，可能的話盡量避免額外的開銷總是最理想的。很遺憾地，我們無法接受你們對於賠償的要求。

從妳的描述中可以很清楚知道問題在哪裡。斷電加上沒有適當關機，機器需要重新開機。如果沒有確切執行，T2000 可能就無法運作。你們所雇用的技師很可能沒有注意到這點。我們建議妳參考機器操作手冊。第一百一十五頁到一百一十九頁詳細說明重新啟動 T2000 的正確程序。我附上了英文手冊讓你們方便查詢。請參閱。

我們理解你們的沮喪。希望我們的建議能有所幫助。引導你們解決使用我們機器所遇到的各種技術問題，是我們職責也是我們的榮幸。相信有了我們的指引你們便能解決問題。如果你們有任何問題或疑慮，請不要客氣，儘管再與我聯繫。

謹上

羅哈利
桃園包裝公司

IV. 電話要求賠償必備句

要求賠償

A: **The cooling unit has broken down,** so we're filing a claim to **replace it.**

冷卻裝置損壞了，所以我們要求更換。

B: **I see. What was the cause of its breaking down?**

我瞭解了。是什麼原因造成損壞的？

....

狀況說明

A: **The product casing** seems to have been damaged <u>in production.</u>

商品外殼好像在製造過程中受損了。

> in production 是指「在生產過程中」，go into production 則表示「投入生產」，即「大量製造」的意思，而 out of production 則表示「停產」，其他說法包括 no longer available、be discontinued。

B: **I don't see how that is possible. It couldn't have made it through inspection.**

我不覺得有那個可能。那樣不可能通過檢測的。

A: **What kind of difficulty have you experienced with our product?**

你使用我們產品時有遭遇什麼困難嗎?

B: **There seem to be a number of defects in the way it was made.**

似乎在製作的方式上有許多缺失。

....

造成損失

A: **Consequently, we've <u>incurred</u> a number of expenses.**

因此,我們蒙受許多的損失。

> incur costs/expenses 表示陷入財務上的困境,incur 的字義是「招致、蒙受」,表示由於某事而導致不好的情況發生。

B: **Expenses for what?**

什麼方面的損失?

....

賠償項目

A: **We would like you to reimburse us for the cost of repairing the machine.**

我們要你們賠償我們修理機器的費用。

B: **I understand, but I'm still not sure that the fault lies on our side.**

我理解,但我還是不確定錯誤是由我方造成的。

V. 用電話要求賠償

Ron: Hello. This is Ron Reynolds. How may I help you?

Sunny: Hello, Mr. Reynolds. This is Sunny Wu from Dragon Decals. How are you today?

Ron: I'm fine. What can I do for you, Ms. Wu? How is that sticker machine we sent you working out?

Sunny: Actually, that's exactly why I'm calling. It has broken down. Apparently, the cutting blade was dull.

Ron: That's strange. It was a new machine. What would you like us to do about it?

Sunny: We've had to pay for a professional to come in and sharpen it. It's working fine now. But we'd like your company to reimburse us for the cost of the sharpening.

Ron: I'm not in a position to authorize that. I'll have to talk to my people.

Sunny: That's fine. You can get back to me once you've had a chance to discuss it with them.

Ron: Thank you for bringing this to our attention.

Sunny: Not at all. It's always a pleasure dealing with your company.

Ron: The feeling is mutual. Until next time, Ms. Wu.

龍之印花的桑妮打電話給貼紙機供應商抱怨機器狀況,希望能拿到修理賠償。

你好。我是榮‧雷諾茲。有什麼我可以幫忙的嗎?

你好,雷諾茲先生。我是龍之印花的吳桑妮。你今天好嗎?

我很好。吳小姐,我可以為妳做什麼嗎?我們送去給你們的貼紙機運作如何?

事實上,我正是為此打來。它故障了。很明顯裁切刀是鈍的。　　狀況説明

奇怪了。那是新的機器。妳希望我們怎麼做?

我們已經花錢請了一位專業人員來把它磨利一點。現在運作起來沒問題了。但希望貴公司能賠償我們磨刀的費用。　　造成損失

賠償項目

這件事我無權決定。我必須跟我們其他人談一談。

沒問題。一旦你有機會和他們討論後,你可以再回電給我。

感謝妳告訴我們這件事。

一點也不會。能和你們公司做生意一直都是我的榮幸。

彼此彼此。再聯絡,吳小姐。

I. 請求技術協助一定要會的句型

✖ PLAY ALL | TRACK 168

句型1 > **遇到問題**

We are currently experiencing a problem with sth. and require . . .

- We are currently experiencing a problem with the mixer and require technical assistance.
  我們最近在攪拌器使用上遇到問題，需要技術協助。

句型2 > **聯絡窗口**

Our order was handled by sb.

- Our order was handled by your sales representative, Mr. Terrence Powder.
  我們的訂單是由你們的業務代表泰倫斯・鮑德所負責。

句型3 推測原因

Our best guess is that . . .

- Our best guess is that there is an internal problem with the motor that drives the mixer.

  我們認為最有可能是啟動攪拌棒的馬達裡頭有問題。

......

句型4 引用條款

The warranty states:

- The product warranty states:

  商品保證書上寫著：

II. 用 e-mail 請求技術協助

To: | Great Grinders

Subject: | Requesting Technical Assistance

Greetings,

遇到問題
Our company purchased a meat grinder from you about eight months ago. We are currently experiencing a problem with the mixer and require technical assistance. We also have a few questions regarding how to proceed.

聯絡窗口
Our order was handled by your sales representative, Mr. Terrence Powder, but we have been unable to reach him by phone or e-mail. Perhaps he could fill you in on the details of our order.

Back to the problem at hand: Not long ago, the grinder's mixing paddles started slowing down. Then, according to the operator at the time, the machine made a strange noise, and it stopped mixing. The other components seem to be fully functional.

推測原因
Our best guess is that there is an internal problem with the motor that drives the mixer.

引用條款
The product warranty states: *"In the event of a malfunction or other complication with the machinery, the client may request technical service within a year of purchase.*

This may take the form of instructions, advice or guidance. If the matter requires the attention of a technician, support may be sent from Great Grinders directly or outsourced to a local company." Given our location, we assume you would prefer that we find a certified technician here and then ask you to reimburse us. Do you know of any in our area, or could you inform us of how to find one?

Finally, we ask that you give us an answer no later than Friday, May 4, if possible. We are currently using our back-up grinder which is considerably slower than yours. This has made it difficult to meet production demands. We look forward to hearing back from you shortly.

Sincerely,

Aaron Hsieh
Magic Meats

中文翻譯

收件人：優良絞碎機

主旨：請求技術協助

您好：

我們公司在大約八個月前向你們購買了絞肉機。我們最近在攪拌器使用上遇到問題，需要技術協助，關於如何進行此事我們也有一些疑問。我們的訂單是由你們的業務代表泰倫斯‧鮑德所負責，但是我們一直無法透過電話或是電子郵件聯絡上他，或許他可以詳盡提供你一些我們訂單上的細節。

回到手邊的問題：不久之前，絞肉機的攪拌棒開始速度變慢。然後，根據那時候的作業員所說，機器發出奇怪的聲音，之後就停止攪拌，其他組件的功能似乎都正常，我們認為最有可能是啟動攪拌棒的馬達裡頭有問題。

商品保證書上寫著：在購買一年內，如有故障或是其他機器引發的問題，客戶可以要求技術服務。服務方式包括操作說明、建議或是諮詢。如果問題需要由技術人員處理，可以從優良絞碎機直接派人協助或是外包給當地的公司。以我們的地點來說，我們猜想你們寧願選擇我們在這裡找到合格的技術人員，然後再向你們求償。你知道在我們這區有沒有這樣的人員，或是能不能告訴我們要如何找到這樣的人？

最後，如果可能的話，我們請求你們在五月四日星期五之前給我們一個答覆。我們目前使用的是備用絞肉機，和你們的機器比起來慢多了。這使我們難以達到生產需求。我們期待盡快聽到你的回覆。

謹上

謝艾倫
神奇肉品

III. 用 e-mail 回覆技術協助請求

✖ PLAY ALL | TRACK 170

To:	Aaron Hsieh
Subject:	Re: Requesting Technical Assistance

Dear Mr. Hsieh,

Thank you for contacting us concerning your problem with the meat grinder we sent you.

Mr. Powder is no longer with Great Grinders, so I will be handling our correspondence from now on. We do have your invoice on file, and you will be pleased to know that the warranty does indeed cover technical assistance in this case.

Finding a technician in your area should not be difficult. The engineering behind our grinders is quite standard in the industry. Any technician certified to service these kinds of machines should be more than capable of handling your problem. We do ask, however, that you get an estimate before going ahead with any repairs.

I understand that you want this issue resolved quickly, so please call me as soon as you know the price of the repairs. That way, I can verbally authorize it for you on the spot. You can find my number below. I will be happy to answer your call at any time of day. Service is our number one priority.

Thank you.

Regards,

Kelly Waite
Great Grinders

——————————— 中文翻譯 ———————————

收件人：謝艾倫

主旨：回覆：請求技術協助

親愛的謝先生：

關於我們寄去絞肉機的問題，感謝你與我們聯繫。

鮑德先生已經不在優良絞碎機服務，所以今後將由我負責處理我們之間的聯繫。我們檔案中有你們的發貨單，而你會很高興知道，保證確實包含了此種情況下的技術協助。

要在你們地區找到技術人員應該不是件難事。我們絞碎機的工程技術是相當符合工業標準的。任何一位提供此種機器服務的合格技術員應該都能勝任處理你的問題。不過，我們必須要求你在進行任何維修前要先拿到估價。

我瞭解你們想盡快解決這個問題，所以請你一知道維修費用就盡快打給我。那樣的話我可以當下口頭允諾你。你可以在信件下方找到我的號碼。一天的任何時段我都很樂意接到你的電話。服務是我們的最高指導原則。

謝謝

謹上

凱莉·維特
優良絞碎機

IV. 電話請求技術協助必備句

✕✕ PLAY ALL | TRACK 171

遇到問題

A: **We've been having some problems with the labeler you sent us.**

你寄來的標籤機我們有一些問題。

B: **That's not good. Can you describe the problem in more detail?**

那不太妙。你可以更詳細說明是什麼問題嗎？

聯絡窗口

A: **We have previously been in contact with Ms. Tina Wu, your Head of Sales.**

我們先前一直是和吳蒂娜，你們銷售部的經理聯繫。

B: **Yes, Ms. Wu. I can <u>refer</u> your issue <u>to</u> her if you'd like.**

是的，吳小姐。如果妳要的話，我可以把妳的問題轉給她。

> refer . . . to sb 表示將某事提交給有權處理的人。

引用條款

A: By the terms of our agreement, we are entitled to free technical assistance.

根據合約條款，我們享有免費技術協助的權利。

B: That's true. We'll do our best to help you handle the situation.

沒錯。我們會盡我們所能來幫你處理問題。

通常客人在請求協助時，都會先引用條款來確定商品在保固期內（warranty period），若在保固期內（under warranty），廠商就必須提供協助，若不在保固期內（no longer under warranty），廠商就沒有辦法提供賠償，而有些商品則是提供終身保固（lifetime warranty）。

一般提供技術協助都是派有照技師（licensed technician），或是廠商授權的授權技師（authorized technician），也可能派客人所在地的當地技師（local technician）以降低交通成本。

推測原因

A: We suspect the problem has something to do with the circuitry.

我們懷疑問題跟電路有關。

B: **That could very well be.**

那是非常有可能的。

> 機器故障可以説 breakdown、malfunction，動詞則可用 break、die、fail、stop working 等來表示，也可以用形容詞 be out of order 來描述故障狀況。
>
> 通常故障時廠商會要求客人參照操作手冊，先維修看看，操作手冊叫 operating manual 或 operating guide，也可説 technical handbook 或 user's guide。規格指南則稱為 specifications manual。

回覆期限

A: **We hope you can give us an answer now or at least by the end of the day.**

我們希望你現在或至少在今天之前可以給我們一個答案。

B: **I can let you know by the end of the <u>workday</u>.**

在今天下班前我會讓你知道。

> 「工作日」還可以用 business day、working day 來表示。

A: **Your time or ours?**

你們的時間還是我們的時間？

B: **Whichever you prefer.**

看你比較希望是哪一個。

V. 用電話請求技術協助

Greg: Hello, this is Greg Lin from the Ice Cream Hut. We bought one of your machines a few months ago.

Wanda: That's right. Hi, Mr. Lin. What can I do for you today?

Greg: Please. Call me Greg. Actually, we've got a problem with the machine you sent us.

Wanda: What kind of problem exactly?

Greg: It's an issue with the dispenser. It doesn't release the ice cream evenly. We haven't been able to fix it ourselves.

Wanda: Alright. What would you like to see from our end?

Greg: We understand that by the terms of our warranty we're entitled to free technical assistance.

Wanda: That is correct. We can't send our own technician over due to the distance, but we can reimburse you for one outsourced from your area.

Greg: Great. That's exactly what I wanted to hear.

Wanda: Do me a favor though and call me while the technician is there so we can maybe suggest ways to keep the cost down.

Greg: Excellent. Thanks a lot.

Wanda: OK. Just call me whenever you're ready.

冰淇淋小屋代表葛瑞格打電話給供應商，詢問機器維修問題是否包括在保證條款中。

妳好。這裡是冰淇淋小屋的林葛瑞格。幾個月前
我們買了你們的一部機器。

沒錯。林先生你好。今天我可以為你做什麼嗎？

請叫我葛瑞格就好。事實上，你們寄來的機器我　　`遇到問題`
們有一些問題。

確切來說是什麼問題呢？

是分配器的問題。它無法將冰淇淋均勻擠壓出　　`推測原因`
來。我們沒有辦法自己修理。

好的。你想要我們怎麼做？

我們知道依據保固條款，我們有權利享有免費的　　`引用條款`
技術協助。

沒錯。由於距離的關係我們沒有辦法派自己的技
術人員過去，但可以補償你們所在地區一位外包
人員的費用。

太好了，這就是我想要聽到的。

但請幫我一個忙，當技術人員到你那邊的時候請
打給我。我們或許可以給一些建議好降低成本。

太棒了。感激不盡。

好的。任何時候你準備好就打給我。

讀友專用訂購單

（請依照以下步驟填寫訂購單，並沿著虛線剪下訂購單傳真，以利客服人員處理訂單）

STEP 1 選擇訂閱方案

☐ Yes！我要自20＿＿＿年＿＿＿月開始訂閱

請勾選要訂閱的雜誌及版本、期數

☐ ABC 互動英語｜初級　　　☐ Live 互動英語｜中級
☐ ALL+ 互動英語｜中高級　　☐ biz 互動英語｜職場
☐ CNN 互動英語｜新聞

※ 訂閱雜誌滿 3 個月，可隨時更換 LiveABC 其他雜誌，不限次數

互動光碟版	課文朗讀版
☐ 1 年 12 期（加送 2 期） 零售價 ~~2,640~~ 元 訂閱優惠價 **1,900** 元	☐ 1 年 12 期（加送 2 期） 零售價 ~~2,160~~ 元 訂閱優惠價 **1,590** 元
☐ 2 年 24 期（加送 6 期） 零售價 ~~5,280~~ 元 訂閱優惠價 **3,600** 元	☐ 2 年 24 期（加送 6 期） 零售價 ~~4,320~~ 元 訂閱優惠價 **2,990** 元

客服電話：**(02)2578-7838**（週一至週五 9:00AM~6:00PM）

STEP 2 填寫訂戶資料

編號：9372C

訂戶資料

姓 名：＿＿＿＿＿＿＿＿＿＿＿＿＿＿＿＿＿＿
寄送地址：＿＿＿＿＿＿＿＿＿＿＿＿＿＿＿＿
聯絡電話：＿＿＿＿＿＿＿＿＿　手機：＿＿＿＿＿＿＿＿
E-mail：＿＿＿＿＿＿＿＿＿＿＿（請務必填寫以利電子報寄送）
☐ 我不願意收到 CNN、Live 互動英語電子學習報
☐ 我不願意收到 LiveABC 互動英語教學集團相關好康活動訊息 EDM

信用卡資料

持卡人姓名：＿＿＿＿＿＿＿＿＿＿＿＿＿
信用卡類別：☐ VISA　☐ MasterCard　☐ JCB
信用卡號碼：＿＿＿＿＿＿＿＿＿＿＿＿＿＿＿
發卡銀行：＿＿＿＿＿＿＿＿　信用卡期限：20＿＿ 年 ＿＿ 月
總金額：新台幣 ＿＿＿＿＿＿ 元 +＿＿＿＿ 元（如需掛號費，每期 20 元）
＝ ＿＿＿＿＿＿ 元整
持卡人簽名：＿＿＿＿＿＿＿＿＿　統一編號：＿＿＿＿＿
抬頭：＿＿＿＿＿＿＿＿＿　發票類別：☐二聯式　☐三聯式

注意事項：訂就送 CNN 互動英語電子學習報 + Live 互動英語電子學習報，訂一年送一年，訂二年送二年。（圖書館不適用此活動）

24 小時傳真訂購專線：**(02)2578-5800 / (02)2578-2707**

國家圖書館出版品預行編目 (CIP) 資料

BIZ E-mail+ 電話英語 /LiveABC 互動英語教學集團編譯.

-- 再版 . -- 臺北市：希伯崙公司 , 民 105.05

　面 ; 　公分

ISBN 978-986-441-057-6(平裝)

1. 商業書信 2. 商業英文 3. 商業應用文 4. 電子郵件

493.6　　　　　　　　　　　　105006388